Mullen, MacLeod and a small crowd of other newsmen were clustered around the newsdesk, on which all the 'opposition' morning papers were spread out. 'Everyone on the Street's asking the same 64,000-dollar question,' said MacLeod, referring to four identical banner headlines that read IS HE A SPY? He held up a fifth, saying, 'Now that's a pearl of a bloody story!' Headlined RED MARKHAM, it featured a photograph taken at a political demonstration in the early fifties. A circle was superimposed to identify Markham amidst a mostly male group marching under a banner with COMMUNIST PARTY OF GREAT BRITAIN printed across it. The story concerned Markham's involvement with the Communist Party before he joined the Labour Party.

DEFENCE OF
THE REALM

Jack Osborne Easton

Based on the original screenplay
by Martin Stellman

Futura

A Futura Book

Copyright © Enigma Films Ltd 1985

First published in Great Britain in 1985 by
Futura Publications,
a Division of Macdonald & Co (Publishers) Ltd
London & Sydney

ISBN 0 7088 3025 0

Typeset in Times by Fleet Graphics, Enfield, Middlesex

Printed in Great Britain by
Hazell, Watson & Viney, Aylesbury, Bucks

Futura Publications
A Division of
Macdonald & Co (Publishers) Ltd
Maxwell House
74 Worship Street
London EC2A 2EN

A BPCC plc Company

Prologue
August 9, 1984

Out of the angry iron-grey clouds high above East Anglia, the lights of two fighter bombers flash like the annunciation of an extraterrestrial invasion. The planes streak through the clouds in tight formation – black, implacable angels of death, carrying B61 bombs under their wings. To the man in the control tower, the blazing lights register merely as benign blips moving towards the centre of his radar screen. Next to the radar screen, a computerized read-out swings into action, displaying an intricate inventory of technical data concerning the two aircraft. A routine message crackles over the radar controller's radio: 'Twenty TFW,' one of the pilots informs him. 'Four Zero One, Information Alpha received. Flight Level seven zero on course Brandon.'

The response, spoken in a syrupy Texan drawl – for the base, like the planes, is American – is the conventional one: 'Four Zero One. We have radar identification. Turn right heading three-three-zero.'

'Four Zero One. Roger.' The plane descends

through the clouds; adjacent to the bombs attached to its wings, a set of wheels fold open, followed by another set of wheels on the opposite wing. At the front of the aircraft, the nose wheel folds open. Inside the brightly lit windows of the control tower, a red light flashes accompanied by a loud buzzer. As relaxed and languid as his colleague in radar control, the tower controller presses a switch that cancels the light and reaches for a fresh stick of gum.

'Four Zero One,' the pilot reports. 'Fully established at five miles.'

'Four Zero One, Roger. Report passing Outer Marker. Surface wind twenty six zero degrees at five knots.'

The Distance From Touchdown indicator shows the plane's distance decreasing from four miles to three.

'Four Zero One, Roger. Outer Marker.'

The radar controller looks out at the runway, the rows of landing lights reflected in the window glass in front of him. He checks the Aerodrome Surface Movement Indicator, a TV monitor linked to a scanner that breaks down the surface area into areas of black for runways and taxiways, and white areas for everything else. Satisfied, he gives the pilot permission to land.

'Four Zero One,' the pilot confirms. 'Cleared to land.'

The sign just inside the permimeter of the high wire

fence that seals the base is barely visible in the twilight.

THIS IS A PROHIBITED PLACE WITHIN THE MEANING OF THE OFFICIAL SECRETS ACT. UNAUTHORIZED PERSONS MAY BE ARRESTED AND PROSECUTED.

On a road outside the fence, running parallel to it, two grimy, desperate-looking teenagers in a blue Ford Sierra are speeding through a driving rain, oblivious to the increasing roar of the approaching plane.

Both boys are wearing green prison overalls. The driver, Steven Dyce, is black, with a small but muscular build and wildly excited eyes. The passenger, Micky Parker, is white, with fair hair and unhealthily pale skin. Parker is trying to tune the car radio to a news programme.

'What you put the bloody news on for?' Dyce asks testily. 'I want music, man, music!'

'Hang on a minute – I want to see if we're on.'

'Ain't no fucking way we'll be on, man.'

'Bet you five quid we are.'

'Five quid?' Dyce snorts contemptuously. 'We ain't got five fucking pee between us.' He reaches for the knob and twists it until hard rock music blasts through the speaker. Above it, both boys hear the wail of a police siren. 'Bastards!' Dyce looks in the rear-view mirror. Flashing headlights and a red light-box proclaiming POLICE-STOP are about a hundred yards behind him and gaining rapidly.

7

'I told you we should never have nicked the motor,' Parker says, looking back apprehensively.

'What fuckin' choice did we have, with the screws right behind us?' Dyce floors the accelerator; if the Ford has any guts, perhaps they can still get away. Awash in adrenalin, he pulls out to overtake the car ahead, then swerves crazily to avoid an oncoming car by inches. The speedometer is passing ninety when he yells, 'Oh, *shit*!' and brakes wildly, nearly losing control of the car. Through the rain he can see the lights of a police roadblock just ahead. The trap seems inescapable until he spots, a few yards before the roadblock, a narrow, unmarked road off to the left. He swings onto it with tires squealing – only to see that it dead ends abruptly at a high wire fence.

'Shit! What the fuck do we do now?' Parker's eyes are wide with panic.

Bringing the car to a skidding halt, Dyce jumps out and heads for the fence. The police car screeches up behind him. 'Come on!' he yells, but Parker is not as quick. The first boy is halfway up the fence when a policeman grabs the foot of the second, who has just started to climb, and drags him to the ground. The policeman mashes Parker's face into the dirt as his partner handcuffs his wrists behind him. Dyce drops to the other side of the fence and runs; silhouetted against the runway lights, he might be an athlete, training for the race of his life.

In the control tower, the noise of the approaching plane is deafening. The tower controller picks up his ringing phone. 'Yup? . . . Okay.' To his colleague he says matter-of-factly, 'We got a Security Condition Amber.'

'Do we have a problem with that?' the radar man asks.

'No. It's over on the outer perimeter.'

The radar controller glances automatically at the TV monitor, then points in alarm. 'We don't have a problem? What the fuck is that, then? The Holy Ghost?'

Panicked, the other man stands up and looks out at the runway. 'Look!' He punches a button that instantly sounds an ear shattering alarm. 'Overshoot! Overshoot!' With helpless horror, both men watch the wheels of Four Zero One touch down on the tarmac of the runway – where the plane's lights catch, just for an instant, the blurred shape of a terrified hunted animal.

Chapter One

Nick Mullen sipped the coffee machine's bitter brew, lit a cigarette and sighed; after three weeks of abstinence, he was a smoker again. In the past he'd been able to blame his lapses, and there'd been dozens of them, on job stress. This time, his only excuse was boredom. He'd been killing time for the past hour, waiting for MacLeod to finish his meeting with Arnold Reece. MacLeod, news editor of the *Daily Dispatch*, was Mullen's boss. Reece, the paper's editor, was MacLeod's boss.

The newsroom was unusually quiet for ten p.m. Leo McAskey, the crime reporter who looked too much like Oliver Hardy for Nick ever to take him seriously, waddled past on his way to the door. 'What's going on in there?' he asked, gesturing toward Reece's office. 'They showing video nasties?'

'Dunno,' Mullen shrugged, 'but Jack told me to stick around till they're finished.'

'Who else is in there?'

'Longman. Champion. Channing. Henderson.'

'Who's Henderson?'

'The company lawyer.'

'You'll miss the pubs, y'know.'

'Thanks for the tip.'

'Better you than me, old son,' said the fat man, hurrying on his way. Mullen pulled some expense account forms out of his desk; he filled in the top lines with great enthusiasm and then remembered, to his annoyance, that the receipts he needed were at home, in his other coat. Stubbing out his cigarette, he picked up a half-finished crossword puzzle.

'Congratulations, dear boy,' a familiar voice said. He turned to see Vernon Bayliss, the *Dispatch's* most senior reporter, standing behind him, holding a copy of the day's paper.

'On my How - A - Million - Pound - Bingo - Win - Changed-My-Life story, you mean?'

'A masterpiece of subtlety and innuendo.'

'My feelings, exactly. What're you on.'

'Battling granny, eighty last birthday, fights off muggers with bare hands and a Sainsbury's carrier bag. Another one for the spike.'

'No one's spiking that. Pride of place next to the Page 3 girl. It's a winner, Vernon.'

'Not when battling granny has a name like Indira Patel, it isn't!'

'I see what you mean.'

'Oh, well,' Bayliss sighed philosophically, 'Take the money and run. Let the buggers upstairs have the sleepless nights.'

The door to Reece's inner sanctum opened and

12

five weary-looking men in shirtsleeves emerged. The one in the lead was MacLeod – a balding, middle-aged Scot with piercing blue eyes. He peered at Bayliss through dirty wire-rimmed spectacles. 'Reece wants to see you. Better take your coat.'

'No peace for the wicked,' said Bayliss, on his way.

Mullen turned back to his crossword puzzle. 'Don't go volunteering for anything.'

'At my time of life, dear boy.'

He moved off, and Mullen turned to MacLeod. 'What's up?'

'It looks as though you and Danny Royce,' said MacLeod, referring to a cameraman Mullen had worked with before, 'will be spending the night together. In Kent.'

Mullen pretended to read from his crossword puzzle: 'Witty, debonair Caledonian news editor, seven letters, begins with M.'

'Cut it out, wise guy, or you'll be covering bingo stories from here on out.'

'Where's Danny?' Mullen asked. He didn't object to working all night when necessary – it was the hanging about that was such a bloody drag.

'In the photo lab, waiting for the final go-ahead.'

'What's holding it up?'

'The threat of a lawsuit. Harry Champion has written a story that's dynamite, but we want to make sure it won't backfire on us.'

'Which is it, Jack – sex or spying?'

'Both, as a matter of fact. An MP and a KGB

13

agent are both involved with a certain Miranda Court. And it isn't just any MP. It's Dennis Markham.'

'Markham . . . wasn't he Chairman of the Commons Select Committee on Defence?'

'Right.'

'Jesus.' Mullen could see the headline already: EX DEFENCE MP IN KGB SEX SCANDAL. With an effort, he suppressed his rising excitement. 'Bigger than bingo, eh?'

Arnold Reece craved order the way some men crave drugs. In every aspect of his life, he strove to be meticulous. His thoughts were precise, his clothes immaculate, his desk top always cleared of everything but absolute essentials. So it was with considerable distaste that he surveyed the residue of the lengthy deliberations that had just been concluded in his office: half-eaten takeaway meals, empty glasses, overflowing ashtrays, crumpled papers. He sighed. Ten minutes with Bayliss and he could go home, where everything, he knew, was clean, and in its proper place.

Bayliss wouldn't be happy about the assignment of course, but any objections would only be a formality. True, this Markham business was rather a special case – Bayliss and Markham went back a long way together – but Bayliss was a company man. He'd been around for far too long to do anything other than what he was told. As for his friendship with Markham – well, contacts were what the newspaper business was all about. Contacts, and grease.

'Come in,' Reece replied to Bayliss's knock. 'Sit down. It's about this story of Harry's.' He handed Bayliss the pages of Champion's article and watched while the older man read it, automatically noting, with disapproval, Bayliss's scuffed shoes, his food-stained tie, his need of a haircut. It was disgraceful the way some men let themselves go to seed after a certain age, he thought. Bayliss had been a damned good-looking man even ten years ago, Reece recalled, always had a way with the ladies, even before his wife died. He was going to fat now, though, and the drink had ruined his face.

Bayliss scanned the pages quickly and tossed them onto Reece's desk with disgust. 'All I want,' Reece said quietly, measuring his words to make the request sound as reasonable as possible, 'is a reaction from Markham to top up the story.'

'So I drew the lucky ticket? This needs more than topping up. It needs standing up. Best bit of muck-raking and unsubstantiated innuendo I've read in years.'

Reece reached into his desk for two glossy 8 × 10 photographs and handed them across to Bayliss, who examined them with visibly shaken assurance. 'Look,' Reece said unctuously, 'I want to give the man a break.'

'And you want me to kindly offer him a noose to put round his neck? Some bloody break,' Bayliss said scornfully. 'Get Harry Champion to do his own dirty work.'

'Vernon, be sensible. You know as well as I do that this story isn't going to lie down and be quiet. You know it won't.'

Bayliss's face reflected his dilemma. In every sense of the word, he was a professional – a newspaperman's newspaperman. He was also Dennis Markham's friend of more than thirty years. Stalling, he lit a cigarette, longing for a drink. 'Who gave you the lead?'

'An unidentified source.' Bayliss flashed him a look of pure scepticism. 'High up,' Reece protested, 'in Intelligence. We've used him in the past and he's always been absolutely reliable.'

'Will he turn up in court if Markham brings an action?'

'Not bloody likely. He'd have to face major charges under the Official Secrets Act if he did. That's why I'm asking you to talk to Markham.'

'There's no hard evidence that Markham and Kleist have actually met,' said Bayliss, trying to postpone the inevitable.

'They're sharing the same tart! They've been photographed leaving her flat on the same evening, within hours of each other!'

'It's circumstantial.'

'Circumstantial? It's about as circumstantial as Pearl Harbor. Look at the photos! First floor flat's for sale. Second floor people were away. Where else were they going? Would you have us put Danny and his camera in bed with her?'

'Has anyone talked to the girl?'

'She'd want at least twenty-five grand up front,

16

and Kingsbrook wouldn't be in to authorize the cheque until tomorrow afternoon. By which time, as you know perfectly well, the opposition will be crawling all over the story. We've got to run it in the morning! Vernon,' Reece said, in a tone of sickeningly sweet reason, 'Surely he'd rather hear it from you than read it over the breakfast table. You'll be able to give him a chance to at least get his act together.'

Bayliss sighed and, as both he and Reece had known he would, capitulated. Filled with self-loathing, he turned his back on his boss, walked out the door and back to his desk. He sank heavily into his chair, dialled the House of Commons and waited, while the years of his friendship with Markham flashed through his mind like time-lapse photography.

Half an hour later, Bayliss was pacing restlessly atop the steps near the Westminster Embankment. The river reflected the lighted windows of the Houses of Parliament, indicating that an all-night sitting was in progress. Bayliss turned his coat collar up against the wind and glanced impatiently from his watch to Big Ben, checking the time. The steps were deserted; the only sound was the traffic. At last he saw Markham's familiar figure hurrying toward him, and moved to meet him.

Markham and Bayliss had been born in the same year – 1920 – but although Bayliss had retained a certain threadbare dignity, he looked a good ten years older than Markham. The MP radiated a quiet sexual vigor and magnetism that, combined with the power of his office, gave him a charismatic presence. 'My dear Vernon,' he said briskly, 'this had better be good. I had to leave just as the Division Bell was ringing. Why couldn't we have met,' he added amiably, 'in Annie's Bar?'

Bayliss braced himself. 'Because this isn't one to shrug off over a few 'g' and 't's, dear boy. I'm afraid it's rather more serious than that.' He hesitated, looking as uncomfortable as he felt.

'Well,' said Markham, still jovial, 'we've had the big build-up. Come on, you'd better tell me!'

'Miranda Court.'

Markham chuckled with relief and bravado. 'Dear, dear, dear. The rag's scraping the bottom of the barrel this time, isn't it? Is that all?' Bayliss said nothing; Markham's warmth turned to wariness. 'Are you talking to me as a friend, Vernon? Or as a newspaperman? Or is that a silly question?'

'Dennis, listen to me . . . '

'Are we on record or not?'

'Dennis, for God's sake . . . I'm trying to help you! Reece thought that if . . . '

'Reece thought he'd the makings of a juicy political scandal,' Markham said, seething, 'so he sent his pimp along to check it out.' Bayliss flinched, cut to the bone. 'I'm sorry. I shouldn't have said that. Look,' he went on, choosing his words carefully, 'you can go back and tell Reece that my private life is my business. And if he tries anything, I'll sue him and Kingsbrook through every damn court in the country!' He started back

18

in the direction of the House, indicating that the discussion was over.

'Dennis.' Bayliss grabbed his arm. 'Dennis – I'm trying to tell you. It's more serious than that.'

Markham turned back, annoyed, and snatched his arm away. 'What the hell are you talking about?'

Bayliss reached for his inside pocket and, pulled out an envelope from which he removed a photograph. He handed it to Markham asking, 'Do you know him?'

Markham studied the grainy enlargement that showed a man in a fur hat, carrying a furled umbrella, getting into a taxi outside Miranda Court's Knightsbridge flat.

'No.'

'You've never met him?'

Markham seemed genuinely puzzled. 'No. What's all this about, Vernon?'

'Miranda Court has other clients.' He tapped the photograph with his finger. 'This is one of them.'

'So?'

'His name is Kleist. Major Dietrich Kleist. Officially listed as a Military Attaché at the East German Embassy. We all know what that's a euphemism for.'

'You mean he's a KGB officer?'

Watching Markham's composure disintegrate, Bayliss was convinced that his old friend was about to be hung for a crime of which he was certainly, but not provably, innocent. The presses were ready to roll – right over Markham's career.

Chapter Two

When the morning papers hit the street, Mullen was sleeping, slumped in the front seat of Danny Royce's car, as soundly as though he were in a feather bed. He looked less appealing asleep than awake, when his personality was sufficiently engaging to divert attention from his lack of conventional good looks. His nose was too crooked, his dark eyes too close together, his black hair too greasy; an hour after a shave, he looked as though he could use another one. He was more bone than muscle, his height slightly less than average. He had a winning smile, though, to which women, in particular, responded – and he wasn't above exploiting it, or anything else that could get him whatever he happened to be after.

At thirty-one Mullen was beginning his third year on the *Dispatch*. He had paid his professional dues in the provinces, first on a weekly, then a daily, covering the usual menial stories – golden weddings, Council meetings and Ordinary Courts cases, of which driving without a license was the most exciting. He wrote the 'Round and About' column of local events, and more than his share of obituaries. His baptism as a general reporter at the *Dispatch* had been even worse – flogging his guts out on bottom-of-the-pile stories, no-go stories, shit stories that nobody ever expected would appear in the paper. It was the standard Fleet Street initiation – a sadistic, demeaning ritual in which news editors paternalistically ensure that young reporters don't get too high an opinion of themselves. First they break you and then, if you prove yourself to be a good, uncomplaining, conscientious Boy Scout, they start giving you some decent stories and treating you with a modicum of respect. Mullen had earned his colours; he'd been smart enough, and keen enough, to play the degrading game. He had even managed to come up with some angles that made the most hopeless stories interesting enough to get them into the paper. He began to get assignments with a bit of potential: covering the Assizes and Crown Courts, interviewing friends and relatives of minor, then major, criminals. During the summer – the so-called silly season, when hard news was scarce – he still had to do some rubbishy stories, such as how some model kept her gorgeous legs in shape by walking her dog, but that was true for all the reporters, it came with the territory. He had no illusions about the quality of either the tabloid or of his work; he knew he was good and getting even better, bingo stories notwithstanding.

Of the three passions that ruled Mullen's life, his

work promised to be the most enduring. The first had been music, the piano – but at sixteen he had realized that his talent was for appreciation, not for performing, and he had given up his dream of a musical career. The second had been Margaret, his estranged and probably soon-to-be-ex wife. Their relationship had been deteriorating before they moved to London; once there, they found that on the rare occasions when they saw each other, they had absolutely nothing to say. Except, of course, recriminations.

During the ten years since they'd met, at a CND demonstration, Margaret had drifted further toward the left, Mullen toward the political cynicism, bordering on nihilism, endemic in his profession. In endless replays of the same argument, he called her friends a bunch of failed hippies, pie-in-the-sky idealists, silly wankers and worse; her response was to call him a smug, self-satisfied, overpaid Fleet Street hack, more emotionally involved with his BMW, bought with the proceeds of padded expense accounts, than with the imminent destruction of the planet. In the end, telling him that their flat wasn't big enough for the two of them and his ego, she moved out. Neither of them had had the heart to file for a divorce; but Margaret had a live-in boyfriend now, and the marriage had become nothing more than a tenuous technicality.

He missed her, but he'd been a loner before he met her, and solitude was familiar, if not always pleasant. If there were times when he felt any sense of emptiness in his life, his work was always there to distract him. There was never a lack of women for sex or for companionship, and it was understood that they were as shy of commitment as he was. He used them, they used him. No problem. He was sociable, but he made sure that nobody got too close. The only exception was Vernon Bayliss.

Bayliss understood about work and obsession. 'Show me a happily married journalist,' he'd said once, 'and I'll show you a lousy journalist.' Mullen hadn't believed in heroes since he was nine years old, but he admired Bayliss more than any man he knew. During more than four decades on the road as a general reporter – never a specialist – Bayliss had covered every important story since D-Day, and was practically an institution on the *Dispatch*. Only the fact that he liked his gin better than it liked him had kept him on the tits tabloid. Even when he was suffering from his monumental hangovers, his copy was always impeccably correct and on time. Mullen had learned a lot from him, mostly by osmosis. They enjoyed one another's company, and often closed up the pub together after work. Like all cynics, both men were closet romantics and shared a 'hope for the best, expect the worst' philosophy. Mullen felt closer to Bayliss than he ever had to his own father.

Mullen shifted position and began to snore softly while Royce, hopelessly wakeful, searched in his camera bag for a cold sausage roll. The car was parked outside Dennis Markham's well-appointed country cottage. As the sky grew light, Royce munched absently on his unappetizing breakfast and switched on the car radio. 'Here again are the main points of the news,' he heard. 'There's been wide-ranging reaction this morning to the newspaper report which alleges the involvement of former Chairman of the Commons Defence Committee, Dennis Markham, with a KGB agent . . . ' Wiping the condensation off the side window, Royce saw what he'd been waiting for: someone had opened the curtains inside the cottage's front window. 'Nick,' he whispered urgently, unzipping the camera case at his feet. Getting no response, he shook him gently, then harder. 'Wakey! Wakey! Liven up, cock. Someone's up and about inside.'

Without opening his eyes, Mullen reached under the seat for his electric razor. Five minutes later, looking rumpled but presentable, the two men approached the front door of the cottage. Mullen rang the bell.

'Good morning,' he said brightly to the attractive young woman who opened the door in her dressing gown. She regarded him steadily with aquamarine eyes, blonde hair rippling down over her shoulders. What the hell was Markham doing with Miranda Court, Mullen wondered, when he had this at home? He smiled, turning on the charm. 'Mrs Markham?'

'No.' Before she could shut the door he put his foot in the way – a practised manoeuvre – and held

24

out his press card. 'I wonder if I could speak to Mrs Markham. Just for a couple of minutes.'

The woman looked him up and down with unnerving directness. 'Mrs Markham is not available for comment.'

'Are you?' he asked. Amused by his cheek, she smiled back. 'No,' she said gently. 'I'm sorry.'

'Can you tell me if she has talked with her husband yet?'

The smile faded. 'I should move your foot if I were you.'

'Look,' Mullen said ingratiatingly, 'right now we're the only ones here. Give us five minutes with Mrs Markham and we personally guarantee to drive you, and her, to wherever you want to go before the circus arrives.'

She looked down at his foot. 'Do you mind?' He shrugged, conceding defeat. 'Thank you.' The door shut firmly.

'I don't like these stories,' Royce said as they walked back to the car. 'Catching people at it. Makes me nervous.'

'You getting soft, Danny?'

'No . . . I just don't like doing people up, that's all. Gimme children and animals, any day of the week. Talking of animals . . . ' He gestured toward an approaching car. 'The *Express* boys are here.' Within minutes, four more cars had created a traffic jam in the quiet lane and a dozen reporters and photographers clustered around the front gate of the cottage, pencils and cameras poised.

'The whole bloody Street's here,' said Mullen.

'All we need now is the *Tunbridge Wells Gazette* and we'll have a full house.' For the first time in weeks, or so it seemed to Mullen, the sun came out. He leaned against Royce's car, reconciled to a long wait.

At exactly half past nine o'clock, a black taxi drew up in front of the gate. 'Here we go!' said Royce, gathering his gear together. The pack of journalistic wolves descended on a woman in raincoat and headscarf who ran out the front door of the cottage toward the waiting taxi, her arm trying to shield her face, stolidly repeating 'No comment' to an absurd litany of questions:

'Mrs Markham, would you care to comment on this morning's news?'

'Will you be talking to your husband in the near future?'

'Do you believe your husband is a spy?'

'Have you met Miranda Court?'

'When will you see your husband?'

'Are you going to London now?'

With a final 'I told you, I have nothing to say,' she got into a taxi. As it pulled away, passing right in front of Mullen the woman looked up and he saw, with a shock of recognition, the same aquamarine eyes that had appraised him so thoughtfully at the door. As the taxi drove off, the other reporters ran for their cars and took off in pursuit of what Mullen knew was a decoy. Grinning, feeling very pleased with himself, he motioned for Royce to get back in the car. When Mrs Markham did emerge, she'd be all his.

Chapter Three

Trudy Markham was a strikingly handsome woman; thanks partly to genetic luck, partly to an iron, self-imposed discipline, she looked a good dozen years younger than her fifty-three years. While she waited for Nina Beckman, her husband's secretary, to throw the wolves off the scent, she applied her makeup carefully. Even with the ground crumbling beneath her, she would keep up appearances.

When the road outside was quiet again, Mrs Markham tucked a stray strand of her ash blonde hair into place, checked her image one last time in a full-length mirror, and rang for a mini-cab. In spite of a sleepless night, she felt no fatigue. Anger, she thought, was an effective source of energy, and this morning she had energy to burn.

The dark-haired young man who politely opened the door of the mini-cab for her said, 'Police, madam. The press have gone,' and flashed an official-looking card at her.

27

'Thank you.' He got into the back seat beside her.

'Station, ma'am?' asked the driver.

'Yes, please. I must say,' she said to the man beside her, 'it's very thoughtful of the police to provide me with an escort.' The mini-cab sped down the road, leaving an admiring Danny Royce in its dust. Mrs Markham fumbled in her handbag for her cigarettes. Ever solicitous, Mullen held out his pack of Dunhills, his other hand ready with a lighter. 'That's very kind of you. I seem to have left mine behind.' She took a long pull and threw her head back on the seat, blowing the smoke toward the roof. 'You're not having one?' she asked.

'I gave up a couple of years ago, actually.'

'But you keep a pack handy for ladies in distress.'

'Yes,' Mullen said, sharing the joke, 'something like that.'

She looked at her watch, then out of the window. Reaching into his pocket, Mullen surreptitiously switched on his microcassette recorder. 'Are you from the local police?' Mrs Markham asked, mildly curious.

'No . . . I'm not.'

'You're not from Scotland Yard, surely?'

'It must have come as a bit of a shock,' he said, ignoring her question.

'That pack of vultures outside? No, I'm used to it. Politicians' wives generally are.'

'No – I meant the news in the papers.'

28

'What do you think?' she snapped. 'Wouldn't you be shocked if your wife had been carrying on behind your back?'

'Probably,' said Mullen, slightly off balance, 'but we're separated. So my wife can carry on with whom she likes.'

'I'm sorry,' she said, embarrassed.

'Did you know about this woman?' he asked, pursuing his advantages.

'When your husband is never at home except at weekends and he also happens to be an MP, you'd have to be very stupid indeed if you didn't make allowances for the occasional brief encounter.' She hadn't meant to say that. She looked nervously at her watch again.

'I mean,' Mullen carried on boldly, 'it's a pretty serious business. The KGB man – Kleist? The newspapers are suggesting that your husband actually knows him.'

'When you are an MP you meet all sorts of people. But I'll tell you one thing, Mr . . . ?'

'Mullen. Nick Mullen.'

'I'll tell you one thing, Mr Mullen. My husband may be an adulterous bastard, but one thing he is certainly not – and that is a Soviet spy. Believe me, I know him.'

'Of course. Still, the papers do have a point. I mean – a former Chairman of the Defence Committee and a top KGB agent – sleeping with the same woman . . . '

'Not at the same time, I presume.' Her voice dripped with acid.

'Perhaps not. But with respect, Mrs Markham, I don't think it's necessarily a question of him being a spy . . . '

'Well, what is it a question of, then?'

'It's a question of his placing himself in a situation where the risk of secrets being passed is unacceptably high.' He knew he was on thin ice now, but would continue until it gave way.

'Oh come, come, Mr Mullen. You think that in the middle of making love to this whore he had an irresistible urge to tell her all about Polaris Subs, Vulcan Bombers, Harrier Jump Jets? Is that it?'

'Well, your husband wasn't exactly anti-Soviet. Wasn't he in the Communist Party at one time?'

For the first time she looked hard at Mullen; he felt the ice giving way. In her eyes, he could see the realization of still another betrayal dawning. 'Who are you?' she asked coldly.

'Did you know he'd been a Communist?'

'You're not the police! You're a reporter! A bloody reporter!'

'Just doing a job, Mrs Markham.'

'Driver! Stop the car!'

One last try, as the car slowed to a halt. 'Will you be talking to your husband, Mrs Markham?'

'It's none of your damned business!'

'You'd be much better off giving me a full statement . . . '

'Get out!'

With nothing to lose, he held out his tape recorder. 'I mean, you might like to clarify some points. For example, you referred to your husband as an adulterous bastard.'

'Get *out*!'

The car deposited him, jubilant with success, on the unpaved country road, and sped away. Within minutes, Royce had picked him up and they were heading to the nearest phone.

Chapter Four

The *Dispatch* carried the story on the front page the next day, under Mullen's byline:

Trudy Markham, wife of MP Dennis Markham, spoke for the first time yesterday about her marriage to the man in the middle of the call-girl spy scandal. Rocked by revelations about her husband's relationship with a call-girl, the ashen-faced Mrs Markham dodged waiting newsmen as she left the couple's £80,000 cottage for London. But later, the attractive fifty-three-year-old broke down and spoke tearfully about her seventeen years of marriage to the prominent left-winger. Referring to her husband as an adulterous bastard, Mrs Markham denied any possibility of Markham being a Soviet spy.

An accompanying story quoted Markham's statement to the press, issued through his solicitors, denying that he had ever met Kleist, the Soviet spy. 'It came as a complete shock to me that he was an acquaintance of Miss Court's, and I can only describe it as an extraordinary coincidence. I have never discussed Defence details with Miss Court, nor anyone else for that matter, even though my involvement in this area came to an end in 1979, when the new government came to power.'

Mullen, MacLeod and a small crowd of other newsmen were clustered around the newsdesk, on which all the 'opposition' morning papers were spread out. 'Everyone on the Street's asking the same 64,000-dollar question,' said MacLeod, referring to four identical banner headlines that read IS HE A SPY? He held up a fifth, saying, 'Now that's a pearl of a bloody story!' Headlined RED MARKHAM, it featured a photograph taken at a political demonstration in the early fifties. A circle was superimposed to identify Markham amidst a mostly male group marching under a banner with COMMUNIST PARTY OF GREAT BRITAIN printed across it. The story concerned Markham's involvement with the Communist Party before he joined the Labour Party.

'I don't want to see the opposition coming up with any more like that. So, Nick, check out where the Markhams go on holiday – Romania, Bulgaria, any Soviet countries – and check out who he met abroad, if he attended any official functions. Oh, and Nick,' he added as the reporter turned away, 'Good piece you did on the wife.' Turning back to the remaining newsmen, he asked, 'Has anyone found Miranda bloody Court yet?'

'O'Shaunnessy's just called. He says she's definitely done a runner, reckons Spain.'

33

'Right,' said MacLeod. 'John, check all flights out of London to Spain in the last forty-eight hours!'

Feeling somewhat deflated, Mullen went to his desk and pulled out his expense sheets, then swore as he remembered again that his receipts were at home. 'Nick,' a woman called from a neighbouring desk, 'Call for Vernon Bayliss on 23. You want to take it?'

He picked up the phone; he and Bayliss often took messages for each other. It seemed an ordinary enough call; a man with an Oxbridge voice and a slight stammer said merely, 'Please tell Mr Bayliss that George returned his call.' With no more than normal curiosity, Mullen left the message on Bayliss's desk and went upstairs to the cuttings library.

An hour and hundreds of cuttings later – Markham had had a long run in politics – Mullen had found nothing more exciting than the predictable landmarks of a typical political career. His first election to the Commons, his second, the third, and so on. His engagement. His marriage. His name mentioned in Parliamentary Diaries. A mini-scandal involving a drunk driving arrest. His membership of the Defence Committee. Mullen leafed through them again, caught by the photo of the radiant young blonde in the engagment story headed TRUDY GETS HER DENNIS. Trudy Markham in happier, hopeful days. The only clip of the faintest interest was quite small, head-lined LABOUR MPs AT PRAGUE PEACE

CONFERENCE. The dateline was Prague, 1979. A tiny piece that might fit somewhere into a puzzle that as yet had no parameters. Mullen took it to the photocopy machine and lifted the flap; there on the glass, forgotten by the previous user, was another cutting. About Markham, but in a completely different context, unrelated to anything else in the file. Intrigued, Mullen photocopied both clips and returned the file to the Librarian. 'Ted,' he asked casually, 'who else has been in today about Markham?'

'Everyone except the bleedin' Gardening Correspondent. Channing was in early this morning, Champion's been in. Even Reece. Oh yeah, and Vernon too.'

The second clip, headed MARKHAM PROBES DEATH OF ESCAPED PRISONER, began, 'Former Minister Dennis Markham has again demanded a new inquest into the death of escaped prisoner Steven Dyce . . . '

Chapter Five

'I still can't help feeling a bit responsible for that bastard of a reporter's story about Trudy,' Nina Beckman was saying to Dennis Markham when she spotted Vernon Bayliss making his way toward them in the crowded restaurant near the House of Commons. 'I wish I'd just kept my mouth shut and slammed the door in his face. Hello, Vernon.' She smiled a greeting. Markham looked up, remote and grim.

'Well,' said Bayliss with false joviality, 'I can see you're pleased to see me.'

'Sit down,' said Markham, coolly polite. 'Are you going to eat something?'

'No, thank you, I've eaten,' Bayliss lied. He'd felt slightly sick ever since seeing Markham's drawn, distraught face on last night's *News at Ten*.

In tight, uncomfortable silence, Nina and Markham picked at their food. 'I've been trying to get hold of you all morning,' Bayliss said tentatively. 'It's a bloody business.' Getting no response, or even acknowledgement, he slogged on. 'I honestly didn't think the newspaper would – '

'My dear chap,' said Markham abruptly, 'It's not your fault. You did all you could, in the circumstances. I don't want you blaming yourself.'

'Hello, Dennis,' said a voice with a strong Northern accent. Bayliss looked round to see Alan Wainwright, longtime veteran of the Labour Party, standing over him.

'Hello, Alan,' Markham said warmly. 'How are you?'

'I'm sorry to interrupt, Dennis, but I just had to come over and say that you've got my support if you need it.'

'That's very kind of you, Alan. Thank you.'

'All the hallmarks of another sordid Fleet Street smear campaign against the Left,' said Wainwright, pointedly ignoring Bayliss. 'If you ask me, they should get hold of every copy of those filthy bloody rags ever printed, set light to the lot and throw Victor Kingsbrook on top.' He moved away; Markham stood up.

'I'm sorry, Vernon, I've got to go. Question Time.'

'Dennis . . . ' Bayliss said helplessly. They shook hands; Markham softened slightly.

'Vernon, I appreciate it. The fact is, I don't want to talk about it. The only thing I'm interested in now is saving my marriage.' Feeling even sadder and more guilty than when he arrived, Bayliss watched his friend walk away, motioned to the waitress, and ordered a large gin. 'How's he taking it?' he asked, turning to Nina.

'What do you think? He's shattered.'

'He asked for it in a way – getting involved with that girl.'

'Are you talking about morals? On that count you could condemn half the Commons . . . '

'And the Lords?'

'Only a quarter. The rest are too old.'

'You've never too old . . . so they tell me.'

'I think Dennis is hoping that by just ignoring it, not rising to the bait, and getting on with being an ordinary MP, it'll all just go away. Oh, God, Vernon, the whole thing's so unreal. One minute I'm the secretary of an ordinary constituency MP, the next minute I'm working for a Soviet Spy.'

Bayliss leaned forward, lowered his voice and spoke confidentially. 'Nina . . . do you think it's possible that . . . for some reason we don't understand yet . . . Dennis has been set up?'

'The thought has crossed my mind. But Kleist would have to be involved in it, wouldn't he? And that doesn't make any sense at all. Kleist is the joker in the pack.'

'I know. Is Dennis getting any support from the leadership?'

'Hah! The leadership was sorely embarrassed and wants no truck with the sordid affair. There's an election coming up, for God's sake! He's been deserted, Vernon.'

'Listen, Nina . . . ' Bayliss leaned close to her and lowered his voice, 'I want you to tell Dennis that I'm doing a bit of digging. I think I may be on to something . . . '

'What?'

'It isn't solid yet. But tell him . . . just tell him to hang on, will you?' Bayliss felt a hand on his shoulder. 'Hello, Vernon,' said Mullen. 'I'm looking for Harry.' He knew perfectly well that Champion was sitting at his usual table, in an alcove near the door; what he wanted was an introduction to the woman he recognized as Trudy Markham's decoy. Today she looked schoolgirlish, almost prim, in a blue dress with demure white collar, hair pulled back into a long plait. Mullen remembered how incredibly lovely she'd looked in the doorway of Markham's cottage – in her dressing gown, slightly dishevelled. But Bayliss clearly had no intention of introducing them.

'He's over there,' he said, waving in Champion's direction.

'Thanks,' said Mullen, undeterred. 'Hello,' he said to Nina, who only glared at him. He nodded, and headed for Champion's table.

'A fellow scribe,' Bayliss told Nina.

'I know. He's the one that wrote that rubbish about Trudy. Bloody disgusting.'

At Champion's table, Mullen ordered a double gin and tonic. He distrusted and normally avoided the smarmy, pudgy-faced Champion, who had even less charm than scruples, but, on occasion, Harry could be quite useful.

'Who's the girl with Vernon?' Mullen asked.

'Nina Beckman. Nice isn't she? Markham's

personal secretary. Vernon has been seeing a lot of her lately. Been in the House quite a bit, too. What angle is he working on, do you know?'

'No idea.'

'He's a bit cut up about Markham. They were great friends. They were in the Spanish Civil War together, y'know.'

Mullen was astonished. 'Vernon was a Communist! He never told me!'

'Probably wanted to keep it under his hat. It's not exactly appropriate to Kingsbrook newspapers, is it?'

'Yeah, but that's going back a good few years now, Harry. I mean, he's not in the Party now, is he?'

The waitress brought Nick his drink. 'Well, you know what they say, Nick,' said Champion, raising his glass. 'Once a Communist, always a Communist. Cheers.'

Chapter Six

'Martinique? Where's that?' Mullen asked the travel agent at the other end of the phone. She was trying ever so hard to be helpful.

'It's in the Caribbean.'

'You sure it wasn't Cuba?'

'No, Mr Mullen, they definitely went to Martinique.'

'Just joking,' Mullen assured her. 'How about last year?'

'They went to Ireland. Stayed with friends. We just booked the flight.'

'Do you have a record of any holidays they've taken on their own?'

'No, it's always for the two of them. Why don't you ask Mrs Markham? She makes all the arrangements.'

'Thank you very much,' he said, ticking her name off on his list.

'Will I see my name in the paper?' she asked hopefully.

'You never know.' He put the phone down,

sipped his cold coffee and lit another cigarette. Glancing down at the photocopy about the Prague Conference on his desk, he dialled the number of the House of Commons and asked for Robert Sawyer. While he waited for them to locate the MP, he saw Bayliss walk into the office carrying his battered old leather case and plastic carrier bag.

'I can connect you now,' the operator said.

'Thank you.' He watched Bayliss remove a microcassette recorder, newly purchased and still in its cardboard box, from the carrier bag. Sawyer came on the line. 'Mr Sawyer,' he said hastily, 'You accompanied Mr Markham on this trip to Prague in 1979. I wonder if . . . '

'You're the sixth bloody reporter who's got onto me today,' Sawyer broke in, 'and I'll tell you what I've told all the others. Any imputation that there was something sinister about Dennis Markham taking part in this conference is ridiculous. We were all there as visiting socialists, exactly the same as the socialists from other NATO countries such as Spain, Italy and West Germany, who also attended. That's all I have to say. Thank you very much.' He slammed the phone down. Mullen slipped the photocopy back into his desk drawer. 'Bought yourself a new toy? he called across to Bayliss.

'Good morning dear boy,' Bayliss said cheerfully. 'I thought it was about time I joined the age of technology. Congratulations, by the way. Seems you beat everyone to the post with your Trudy Markham story.'

Mullen watched him struggle to insert the tiny cassette into the pocket-sized recorder. 'A guy named George called,' he said, fishing. 'Did you get the message?'

'Yes, thanks,' said Bayliss, refusing the bait.

'Wouldn't give a surname.' No response. 'Bloody hell, Vernon,' said Mullen, watching him fumble with the machine, 'forget the age of technology, you haven't even caught up with the Industrial Revolution.' With affectionate exasperation he walked round to Bayliss, reached for the cassette and put it in properly. 'I hear you know Markham pretty well,' he said, trying a different bait.

'Where did you hear that?' Bayliss fiddled with the batteries.

'No secrets on the Street of Shame, dear boy. I thought you might be able to give me a few tips.' Bayliss picked up the microphone suction device used for recording telephone conversations and tried to plug the lead into the wrong socket. 'Vernon,' said Mullen, pointing, 'it goes in the other one.'

Bayliss looked at him intently; they knew each other too well to play games. 'So they've got you at it as well, have they?'

'Yeah. So, what's *your* angle?' Bayliss appraised him, cool and inscrutable. He tried again. 'Someone left a cutting behind on the photocopier . . . '

'Listen, Nick,' Bayliss said, friendly, but firm as granite. 'Nothing personal, but why don't you do your story and I'll do mine. All right?'

43

'Like that, is it?' said Mullen.

He was irritated, and a bit hurt. Had Bayliss who had always supported and encouraged him suddenly become a competitor? Didn't Vernon trust him?

'It's like that,' Bayliss said flatly.

'Okay, Vernon, please yourself.' Mullen started back to his desk.

'Nick!' Bayliss called after him. He looked back. 'I'll give you one tip. Tread carefully. Tread very carefully.'

Bayliss reached for his ringing phone. 'Yes? George? Yes sorry I wasn't in . . . '

Mullen saw him lick the suction device through which the little recorder picked up phone conversations. He pressed it onto the receiver, forgetting to push the red RECORD button on the machine. Nick reached over, pressed it for him and walked back to his desk, trying to fathom Bayliss's remark. Passing McAskey, just arrived in the office, Mullen asked automatically, 'How was Grimsby?'

McAskey dropped his briefcase on his desk. 'Twenty-four hours in Grimsby and a man can forget where his appendage is.'

'I thought you'd forgotten already.'

'Yeah, yeah . . . very funny. You seen this Miranda Court bird?' Out of the corner of his eye, Mullen saw Bayliss get his coat and leave hurriedly. McAskey tossed a copy of *The Standard* on Mullen's desk. The headline over a photograph of a glamorous blonde read THE OTHER WOMAN.

44

'Darlin',' McAskey went on, 'as far as I'm concerned, you can have the plans for the entire Western defence system with pleasure.' He pulled out some receipts, bills, and a blank expenses form. 'Christ,' he murmured, looking at one restaurant bill, 'it cost me eighty-two quid for a dinner for two. Think they'll wear that upstairs?'

'Not if it was Grimsby, mate.' Mullen reached for his ringing phone. The man's voice came from a call box; Mullen heard the pips, and the money going in. 'Nick Mullen?'

'Yup.'

'I have some information to give you regarding Dennis Markham.'

'Oh yeah?' Mullen replied cynically; he'd had dozens of similar calls during the course of his career – almost invariably from cranks, a waste of his time.

'Have a look at the 1979 World Peace Council in Prague,' the caller said. That got Mullen's attention.

'Who is this?'

'I wouldn't worry about that. I know what I'm talking about.'

'I've already looked at it,' Mullen said.

'There is a photograph.'

'Who is this?' Mullen repeated, urgently now. The line went dead. He put the phone down and walked over to the newsdesk. 'Anybody just put through a call to me?' The men and women at the phones looked at him and at each other, shaking their heads. On the other side of the newsdesk, a

45

weedy looking man with a moustache was sifting through photographs with his assistant, deciding which would be used for the next day's edition. 'Terry,' Mullen said to the picture editor, 'Dennis Markham. Prague. World Peace Council, 1979.'

The picture editor reached across the desk for a folder bulging with photos and handed it to Mullen. 'If it's not in that little lot, we haven't got it. And, Mullen . . . Let's have 'em back this time, will ya?'

'Terry,' Mullen said reproachfully, 'have I ever let you down?'

Dozens of photos later, Mullen decided that the anonymous caller was probably a crank after all. He'd looked at photos of Markham sitting, standing, walking his dog, making speeches, dedicating buildings – doing everything, it seemed, except attending the conference in Prague. 'That's everything on file?' he asked, returning the folder. 'The picture quality doesn't matter.'

'On our files, yeah. Try the picture library. Might be some unusable stuff there.'

In the picture library, its walls covered with Page three tear sheets, Mullen looked on as the archivist searched through the cabinets of negatives and prints. There must be a million photographs in here, he thought, all meticulously catalogued and easy to find – if only you knew where to look. 'Maybe it's cross-filed,' he said, hope ebbing.

'I've looked under Markham and Prague and

Sawyer,' the archivist said, slamming the file drawer shut.

'Okay,' Mullen said wearily. 'Thanks for trying.'

'I hate to give up. Let's have a look at the cutting.'

Mullen handed him the photocopy. 'Brezhnev!' the librarian whooped triumphantly. 'On the first day,' he quoted from the article, 'the conference was attended by Leonid Brezhnev!'

The photo was there, neatly labelled: *Prague, 1979.* In the foreground, Brezhnev hugged the Czech leader in a Russian-style greeting. Through a magnifying glass, Mullen examined the men in suits behind and around them in various postures of applause. Three of the men he identified immediately as left-wing British politicians. One of the three, standing directly behind Brezhnev and clearly conversing with the man on his right, was Dennis Markham. The man on his right, shown in three-quarter profile, couldn't be positively identified – except, perhaps, in a blow-up of the photo.

In the darkroom, Mullen stood expectantly in front of the tank of developer, watching an image form on a sheet of exposed photographic paper. The image was very grainy at first, almost abstract – a configuration of dots. As Mullen watched, it formed itself into eyes, nose and a laughing mouth. A face, blown up from a much smaller image.

The technician picked the photograph out of the developer with his tweezers, dropped it into the fast-fix solution and then into the wash, where it swilled around with photos of Margaret Thatcher, the Princess of Wales, a Page Three Girl and a puppy with a budgerigar on its head. Finally, he hung it on the drying line, next to where several variations of another blow-up were hanging: the two-shot of Markham and the unidentified man at the Prague Conference. Mullen studied them all minutely, comparing the man at the Conference, with the photo of Dietrich Kleist, outside Miranda Court's flat. Unquestionably, the man sharing the joke with Markham in Prague was Kleist. The caller was no crank.

Chapter Seven

Bayliss sat alone in the unaccustomed silence of the deserted newsroom waiting for Mullen, badly wanting a drink. At midnight, the first edition had been put to bed; the cleaners hadn't arrived yet. For the umpteenth time, Bayliss mentally whipped himself for leaving the incriminating clipping on the photocopying machine. To anyone but Mullen, it might have seemed simple carelessness, nothing worth noting. Mullen, though, had the instincts of a born investigative reporter, and his antennae were fully extended now. Ironically, Bayliss himself had helped Mullen to sensitize those antennae. Explore every lead, he'd taught him, no matter how silly or insignificant it seems. You've got to collect all the pieces before you can tell which ones fit.

Bayliss took an almost paternal pride in the young reporter. He reminded Bayliss of himself at that age – desperately keen on his work, and better than good at it. He had more bottle than Bayliss had ever had, though. He hadn't the weaknesses, the capacity for self-delusion that had impeded the veteran newsman's progress from general reporter to specialist, from tits tabloid to first-rate newspaper. Mullen would never allow his feelings to cloud his professional judgment and lead him down the slippery slope on which Bayliss had embarked in the Markham affair. Mullen was a loyal friend, but he wasn't a fool.

Mullen emerged from the darkness, his footsteps echoing in the empty corridor. Bayliss rose to meet him. 'You'd better take a look at that, Vernon,' said Mullen, handing him an envelope.

Bayliss opened it and took out three photographs. One was the *Prague, 1979* photo. The second was the blow-up of the portion showing Markham and Kleist; the third, the even larger blow-up of Kleist's face. Bayliss studied each one carefully while Nick paced nervously back and forth in front of him. Bayliss's face betrayed only mild perplexity; inwardly, he was reeling. 'Where did you get the original?' he asked, stalling for time.

'What does that matter?'

'Another anonymous source?'

'That's not the point!'

'Okay . . . so what do these prove?'

'They prove,' Mullen said, agitated, 'that your friend is lying! He said categorically that he had never met Kleist.' He pointed to the photographs. 'That's Markham – that's Kleist! You can't argue with that!'

'Isn't it possible,' asked Bayliss, grasping at straws, 'that Kleist was just another face in the crowd? That Markham had no idea who he was?'

'Come on, Vernon. That would be one hell of a coincidence, and you know it.'

'It still doesn't prove,' Bayliss argued, 'that Markham is a Russian agent.'

Torn between his reporter's instincts and his respect for Bayliss's judgment, Mullen hesitated. 'You can't use it, Nick,' Bayliss said, pleading. 'If you do, he'll be crucified!'

'Hang on,' said Mullen hoping to convince himself as well as Bayliss. 'For four-and-a-half years the guy was Chairman of the Commons Select Committee for Defence, during which time he had access to our most important defence secrets. He shares his lover with a known KGB agent. And the same KGB agent happens to be laughing at some joke with him at a conference in Czechoslovakia. Vernon, I *have* to use it!'

Bayliss played his strongest card: his credibility with Mullen. 'Dennis Markham,' he said with absolute certainty, 'is not a traitor.'

'I see,' Mullen shot back sarcastically. 'One old Comrade sticking up for another, eh?'

Taken aback, Bayliss could only stammer, 'What?'

'You heard.'

Bayliss flushed angrily. 'So the dark secret is finally out, is it? Yes, I was in the CP with Dennis. But I left the party in 1956, for God's sake! I should have realized that it's like having a bad dose of the clap – you can never quite get rid of it.'

'Then you're in no position to be objective about it, are you?'

'Hah! Objectivity being the hallmark of this great and honourable newspaper! Spare me the humbug, dear boy!' Bayliss studied the photographs again, playing for time. 'Look, Nick,' he said, placatingly, 'try to understand. I met Markham in 1937, in the Basque country. I was eighteen years old, and terribly ambitious. I was working for the Brighton *Evening Argus* – it was my first job – and I thought my editor would be impressed if I asked him to let me cover the Civil War. I never expected to be actually *sent* there.

'Markham was a student at Cambridge; he'd signed up for the International Brigade. After Spain, we both joined the Party. It was the thing to do for people like us.'

'Like what?'

'It's just a bloody cliché now, but at the time, we had convictions. Consciences. Commitments.' Mullen shot him a sceptical look. 'You think your cynicism is better, do you? What do *you* stand for, Nick? Decency? Justice? Freedom? The dignity of man?'

'What the hell *can* you stand for on a newspaper with five million readers whose deepest convictions are tits and arse, prizes and personalities?'

'Brilliant! Persuade yourself you're doing it because it's what the readers want! That excuses it all, doesn't it? The hypocrisy, the lies, the trivia and it's all right, because it's what the readers

52

want! I'll tell you what you stand for, Nick. You stand for your fourteen grand a year, for your weekly expenses, your annual ski-ing holiday, maybe the fleeting glory of a front-page byline and that's it, everything else can just go to hell!'

'And what makes you so fucking different? Fighting in the Spanish Civil War? Are you saying you haven't made compromises?'

'Christ, no! I've been a champion at compromise. There were always plenty of excuses – the children, the mortgage, the dry rot to take care of, the new Granada, some bloody excuse. I did it for years – but at least I knew it was wrong. I was always ashamed of it. And now I've run out of excuses.'

Nick gave him a searching look. 'Are we still talking about the Markham story? Because if we are, nothing you've said changes the fact that it's a bloody good story.'

'Well,' Bayliss said derisively, 'don't let the truth get in the way of a good story!'

Apparently at an impasse, they looked at each other in silence. Mullen felt his resolve weakening. He trusted Bayliss as he trusted no one else but he sensed that the older man, for God knew what reason, was holding something back. Confused and angry, he jabbed his forefinger at Bayliss. 'Do you know something that I should know? Are you on to something? 'Cos if you are, you'd better tell me now.'

Bayliss sank heavily into his chair. 'I can't. Not yet. I need a few more days.'

53

'A few more *days*!'

'Twenty-four hours. Give me twenty-four hours!'

Mullen sat on the edge of the desk, considered his options, and concluded that he hadn't any. He knew, and so did Bayliss, that if the story didn't appear in the next issue of the *Dispatch*, the anonymous tipster would simply feed it to another paper. 'Jesus Christ,' he said helplessly, 'I can't sit on this. I can't,' he repeated, seeing Bayliss's accusatory look, 'even if I wanted to.'

Acknowledging defeat, Bayliss rose and reached for his coat. 'Tread carefully,' he cautioned. 'Tread very carefully.' Longing for a drink, he walked toward the lift.

Mullen pondered the remark; Bayliss had given him the same mysterious warning during their earlier discussion of the Markham story. Perhaps he was developing a penchant for drama in his old age. Slowly, deliberately, Mullen opened the top drawer of his desk, took out a clean sheet of paper and threaded it into his typewriter. He took off his jacket, draped it over the back of his chair, and started to type.

The sky was getting light as Mullen read through his copy one final time. He added a paragraph: 'Again we ask the question, how could such a man come to hold the politically sensitive position of Chairman of the Commons Select Committee on Defence?' He sighed, mentally replaying his conversation with Bayliss. He couldn't help admiring the man's loyalty to his old friend, but surely his attempt to prove Markham's innocence was merely whistling in the dark. Markham was clearly guilty as hell; the photo proved it.

He got up, awkwardly massaged his knotted shoulders, stretched, and fumbled in his trousers for a 10p piece for the coffee machine. A shot of caffeine, he thought was what he needed. Carrying his cup back from the vending machine to the empty office, a metallic noise stopped him dead in his tracks. Through the shadows he could see, at the end of the room, two burly figures hunched around Bayliss's desk, apparently trying to break into it. 'Oi!' he yelled, running in their direction. The men sprang into action, sprinting out of the room and down a corridor that led to the print shop. Mullen ran after them, in his excitement forgetting the hot coffee that spilled all over his hand and shirt. The men were out of sight, but their footsteps loudly announced their route. Mullen chased them down the corridor and along a catwalk suspended over the empty press room. Two floors below, he heard a door slam and, after that, no more footsteps. He took the stairs two at a time, reaching the door winded and confused. Outside the door was the loading bay. Rumbling conveyor belts were carrying piles of newspapers to lorries waiting at each of a dozen bays. Full lorries were leaving, empty ones arriving. The air was thick with exhaust fumes.

He could see the men running toward the street, dodging the traffic; one glanced back over his shoulder, but he was too far away for Mullen to distinguish his features. Mullen forced his body to run to the road; his chest was on fire. A lorry barely missed him; its driver shouted 'Get out the way, you wanker!' and gesticulated wildly. He stopped, panting and perplexed; the men were nowhere in sight. 'Christ,' he wondered remembering the size of the burglars – if that was what they were – 'what the fuck would I have done if I'd caught 'em?'

Chapter Eight

Mullen had felt the familiar secret thrill when he saw his byline under the next morning's front page headline, THE MP AND THE SPY. The story made him the man of the hour, as he'd known it would. At a celebratory long lunch in the pub, nobody was quite sober; everybody wanted to buy him a drink. He sat at the bar between MacLeod and McAskey, feeling the gin he'd drunk on an empty stomach and wondering why he wasn't enjoying himself more. The normally sweet taste of accomplishment had a faintly metallic edge.

'Another drink?' MacLeod asked, grabbing his glass.

'Yes, thanks . . ' Mullen felt an arm on his shoulder. 'Congratulations,' said Harry Champion. 'Smashing piece, Nick. Smashing! You deserve a drink!'

'Thanks,' said Mullen, 'I've already got one.' He waved at Bayliss, sitting alone at a table across the room, but Bayliss ignored him. McAskey, feeling no pain, was regaling himself, if not his audience, with yet another tale of his romantic adventures, more fantasy than fact. Mullen turned his attention to the television set over the bar. Through the smoke, he saw the face of ITN's News announcer; over the noise of the rowdy celebrants, he heard her voice:

' . . . and now we go over to Gordon Reece Jones at Labour Party headquarters where Mr Markham is just about to make a statement about this morning's developments.'

The words drew the attention of all the newsmen – except McAskey, who babbled on, oblivious.

' . . . Right? She's the one whose husband was sent down for eight years for GBH. So there's me sitting on the sofa, notebook in hand, and in she comes in this see-through nightie thing, telling me how lonely she is. So, I came right out with it. I said . . . '

'Shut up, Leo, I've heard it before,' Mullen snapped, his eyes riveted to the television screen. Markham and his wife were making their way with solemn deliberation to a table with a microphone on it, while motor-driven cameras and flash guns fired away at them from all directions. The television camera moved in on the couple's faces. Trudy Markham's was a study in humiliation; Markham's was dark with shame, guilt, regret. Both seemed to be straining for composure.

'Ladies and gentlemen,' Markham began, subdued but with unexpected dignity, 'Thank you very much for coming this morning. I've prepared a brief statement . . . ' He paused then began to read from a sheet of paper held in an unsteady hand. 'In spite of my repeated and emphatic assurances regarding the alleged relationship with Major Kleist, press speculation and innuendo have continued unabated, culminating in an article which appeared in a national newspaper this morning.'

The newsmen in the bar whistled and cheered a chorus of self-congratulation; Mullen felt someone slap him on the back. 'In view of the damage which this is doing to both the Parliamentary Party and the constituency,' Markham went on, 'I cannot in all conscience continue to serve as its Member. I have therefore decided . . . ' he faltered, took a deep breath and resolutely carried on . . . 'to inform the Speaker of my decision to resign my seat in the House.'

Markham gathered up his papers, stood up, took his wife's arm and started to move off, pursued by a barrage of questions. 'I'm sorry,' he told the reporters, 'but I'm not answering any questions. Thank you.' Like mourners leaving a wake, the Markhams walked away.

Mullen was suddenly sober, feeling the impact of what he had done. Cause and effect: his words on paper, two shattered lives. He pushed the feeling away; he'd only been doing his job. Around him, colleagues downed their drinks and headed back to their typewriters and phones. Bayliss still sat at his table alone, sozzled and silent. It always pained Mullen to see the man he so respected show so little respect for himself. Better get him home, he thought, before he passes out. He walked over to his table. 'Mind if I join you?'

'It's a free country,' Bayliss said blearily. ' . . . I think.'

'You're doing well,' said Mullen, indicating the table of empty glasses and Coke bottles. Unsteadily, Bayliss held up a glass half-filled with a clear liquid and poured some Coke into it.

'Let us give thanks to this splendid beverage,' he said, slurring his words. 'Vodka and Coca Cola! The marriage of capitalism and communism. Detente in a glass!' He turned toward a man in a leather jacket sitting a few tables away, chatting to a woman, and raised his glass. 'Cheers!'

'Who's that?' Mullen asked, mystified.

'Who?'

'Him – the guy you just raised your glass to.'

'Oh, him. That, dear boy, is our friendly neighbourhood spook. Special Branch, y'know. Been following me for days . . . ' He raised his voice, ' . . . haven't you, old cock? Just like a faithful and very stupid dog.' Bayliss drained his glass, got to his feet and took a shaky step in the direction of the leather jacket. 'Come on! Time for exercise! Mustn't sit around all day, must we?' He lurched onto the table, sending the glasses and cans flying.

Mullen took his arm. 'Come on, Vernon, I'll get you home.'

'I don't want your *fucking* help!' Bayliss pulled his arm away.

Mullen was alarmed. Bayliss was normally a peaceful drunk – sometimes happy, sometimes maudlin and weepy, but never hostile. He reached for his arm again, prepared for a scene – but this time, Bayliss offered no resistance. 'Okay,' he mumbled, clinging to Mullen for support. 'I'll come quietly.'

At the door, Mullen turned for another look at the man in the leather jacket. He seemed completely absorbed in conversation with his lady friend. Mullen pondered his friend's uncharacteristic behaviour. Was the drink starting to make him a bit paranoid? With some difficulty, he got Bayliss out of the pub and into a taxi. Mullen, never paranoid, didn't think to look back as the taxi pulled out into traffic and a man in a leather jacket sprinted towards a brown Cortina waiting at the kerb.

Chapter Nine

By the time the taxi had made its way through the heavy afternoon traffic to Notting Hill Gate, Bayliss was snoring, his head on Mullen's shoulder. Mullen paid the driver and half-shoved, half-carried Bayliss into his building. In the lift, Bayliss started apologizing for his behaviour. 'No need to trouble yourself, dear boy,' he said groggily. 'Go on home, I'm fine. Jus' fine.'

In the hallway outside his front door he stumbled and would have fallen if Mullen hadn't caught him. He fumbled with his keys, trying one, then another. 'I'll do it,' Mullen said, taking them from his swaying friend. He opened the door, switched on the lights in the sitting room – and stood speechless with shock. Behind him, in the hallway, Bayliss still fumbled with his keys. 'Vernon,' he murmured, 'you'd better come and have a look at this.'

The room had been thoroughly, efficiently ransacked: books, cushions, papers, pictures, items of clothing and overturned furniture covered the floor. Bayliss surveyed the mess and turned white as a sheet. He was trembling with anger.

'Are you still sober enough to call the police,' Mullen asked, 'or shall I?'

Bayliss didn't answer; he stooped to pick up two of the picture frames that were scattered on the floor. One was a colour family photograph, taken in the mid-sixties, of himself, his wife, son, daughter-in-law and grandchild in a neat suburban garden. The picture glass was cracked. The other, black and white, showed him as a strikingly handsome young man, circa 1940, arm-in-arm with the equally handsome woman he had just married. Mullen picked up another picture frame; in it, a laughing Bayliss and another reporter, both wearing the World War II pressman's 'uniform' of trench coat and hat with Press Card stuck in band, held up two corners of the *Evening Chronicle* on V-E Day. IT'S PEACE, the headline blared.

Bayliss stumbled over to a corner of the room, where a desk remained upright. The bottom drawers, both equipped with locks, had been forced open. Bayliss reached into a small drawer at the top and extracted an old railwayman's timepiece. 'Look,' he said bemusedly. 'A gold watch. Early Victorian. It was my grandfather's! Worth over two hundred pounds!' He pulled out some more items. 'Two gold rings, my mother's and father's. Look, this one's inlaid with rubies.'

'Hadn't we better call the police,' Mullen asked, 'Before you go touching things?'

'The police?' Bayliss echoed mockingly, 'they've been and gone, the bastards!' From another small drawer he extracted an envelope and checked its contents. 'Fifty pounds in cash,' he said, waving the notes at Mullen. 'A birthday present for my grandson. None of it's been touched! It wasn't valuables they were after . . . '

'What were they after, then?' Mullen asked, bewildered.

'Not "they" – not "they"! Give the bastards their proper name. The Special Branch. The Spooks.'

Through the haze of alcohol, Bayliss knew what the intruders had been searching for. He rushed past Mullen, back out the front door of the flat and down the stairs that encircled the lift. He stopped at the first landing and peered intently up into the lift shaft.

'Vernon!' Mullen called after him, 'What the hell are you doing?' Following Bayliss into the corridor, he saw him standing on the landing. 'Vernon! Will you *please* tell me what the *hell* is going on?'

Wordlessly, Bayliss made his way back up the stairs and pushed past Mullen to his door. 'Look, if you're in some kind of trouble,' Mullen said, feeling a twist of pity for his friend, 'I want to help.'

Bayliss spun around to face him. 'Your help has been invaluable,' he said bitterly. 'I'm sure Dennis Markham appreciates all you've done.'

Stung by the sarcasm, stunned by the accusation,

Mullen nonetheless tried again. 'Listen . . . Last night, after you left the office, a couple of . . . '

'Nick,' Bayliss said brusquely, 'just do me a favour. Leave me alone, okay?'

Before Mullen could reply, Bayliss had slammed the door between them.

Bayliss searched the shambles of his flat for a drink, finally finding a flask of vodka in the pocket of an old coat. He took a healthy swig from it, sank into an armchair in the centre of the room, and tried to clear his clouded brain. Did the devastation around him represent a victory, or a defeat? On the one hand, they hadn't found what they were searching for; he was dead certain of that. On the other hand, he knew they wouldn't give up that easily; surely this was only the beginning. And the undeniable truth was that however admirable his intentions, he had neither the resources nor the expertise to take on the Special Branch single-handed. He must have been mad to think that he could.

Maybe, he thought idly, he *was* mad. Otherwise, why wasn't he frightened? He'd buggered this up, he thought, just as he'd buggered up everything else in his life. He contemplated his past and his present and saw only failures. He tried to contemplate his future. He could see no future. I waited too long, he thought – you can't spend a lifetime selling your principles for a few lousy pieces of silver and then expect to redeem yourself with one big flash gesture. He had failed his wife, who had ultimately turned to other men for what he hadn't been able to give her. He'd failed his son, who only found him an embarrassment. He'd squandered whatever talents he'd had in the name of . . . what? Comfort? Survival? Ball-less Bayliss, he called himself, wallowing in self-pity.

He took another generous swig from the flask, leaned his head against the back of the chair and let his eyelids close of their own weight. He felt himself slipping into the twilight anteroom of unconsciousness. It's all too much to cope with tonight, he thought; I'll deal with it tomorrow. Maybe even ask Nick to help me. Tomorrow . . .

He heard the men enter the room, but his eyelids had turned to cement. All you have to do, he told himself, is keep your mouth shut . . .

66

Chapter Ten

Mullen was resilient; he awoke the next morning feeling unaccountably good. He shaved and dressed to the accompaniment of a Fats Waller record and arrived at the office early, relieved that the Markham story, with all its sticky ramifications, was behind him. He still felt outraged by the vandalization of Bayliss's flat, but he was sure that Bayliss, after some sober reflection, had reported it to the police. Vernon might not even remember having thrown him out of his flat – when he was sufficiently pissed, his memory sometimes went on holiday – but if he did, he'd be full of remorse and apologies. Mullen was anxious to talk to him and get it sorted out.

From the street outside the *Dispatch*, he could hear the rhythmic banging of metal on metal that signified a ritual 'Printers' Farewell' for some retiring typesetter. He walked into the press room and joined in, banging a block of type along with the rest, shaking the hand of the embarrassed but pleased retiree, enjoying the camaraderie. A few other reporters, including McAskey, had come downstairs for the ceremony. McAskey yelled something at him, his voice drowned out by the din. He tried again, with the same result. Finally he scribbled something on a piece of paper, scrunched it into a ball and tossed it to Mullen. 'MacLeod wants to see you in his office,' it said. Mullen wondered what his new assignment would be.

He made his way through the crowded newsroom, busy with the first edition, to the glass-partitioned offices at the back. He could see MacLeod, Reece, and a uniformed police officer. He knocked and opened the door without waiting for a reply. 'Come in, Nick,' MacLeod said. He looked worried. 'This is Sergeant Ross.'

Mullen shook Ross's hand and looked expectantly at MacLeod.

'Bad news, I'm afraid,' the Scotsman said. 'It's about Vernon.'

'What about him?' Mullen asked, alarmed by MacLeod's tone.

'He was found dead in bed this morning. Looks like it was a coronary.'

Mullen started at MacLeod incredulously, then slumped, dumb-struck, into a chair. It must be some bizarre practical joke. It couldn't be true. But MacLeod's sombre expression told him it was no joke. 'The Sergeant wants to ask you a few questions,' he said gently, 'Is that okay?'

Mullen couldn't speak.

'Is that okay, Nick?'

Ross took a seat opposite Mullen, appraising

him with eyes like ice cubes. 'I understand you took Mr Bayliss home from the pub yesterday . . . ?'

Mullen stared at the floor and nodded again, still trying to absorb the information.

'How was he?'

'He was fine,' Mullen said, 'absolutely fine.' Compared to being dead, he thought.

'He'd been drinking?'

'Yes, that's what you do in pubs.'

'But he had been drinking?'

'Yes, he'd had a few. We all had.'

'A "few" can mean two or twenty, Mr Mullen.'

'Jesus Christ!' Mullen exploded, 'What is this, the fucking Temperance Society?'

'Steady on, Nick,' said MacLeod. 'The man's just trying to do his job.'

Ross leaned back in his chair, sipping a cup of coffee, watching Nick like a stalking cat. Measuring. Calculating. Waiting. 'Did anything unusual happen?'

Mullen tried to organize his thoughts. He remembered the violation of Bayliss's flat, the brutal destruction of his things. *A heart attack?* What kind of game were they playing? He looked up warily, meeting eyes he instinctively knew not to trust. 'No,' he said curtly, and looked away.

'Are you sure?'

He thinks I know something I don't know, Mullen thought. *What is it? Who is he?* 'Yes,' he said, 'I'm sure.'

'Anything you'd like to add, sir?' Ross's voice was as impersonal as the Speaking Clock.

'No.'

'Fine,' said the sergeant, expressionless. 'Thank you very much.'

Still dazed, but with his mind racing, Mullen rose and made for the door. He heard Reece's voice behind him: 'The funeral's on Thursday, Nick.'

Dazed, Mullen walked to his desk and, without thinking, reached for his expenses form. He stopped, remembering Bayliss's words. *You stand for your fourteen grand a year, for your weekly expenses, your annual ski-ing holiday . . . everything else can just go to hell!* The sight of Bayliss's desk gave him a pang; he couldn't believe that the familiar figure wouldn't walk in any minute, grinning wryly, saying, 'Got you going this time, didn't I, dear boy?'

MacLeod's voice broke into his reverie: 'We all felt the same way about Vernon.'

'Yeah.'

'A good newspaperman.'

'Christ,' Mullen said, shaking his head, 'I don't understand it, Jack! I figured his liver was gone, but . . . his heart?'

'Well, he was no spring chicken, Nick. A man can only take so much.'

Mullen looked up. 'Jack . . . Vernon was definitely up to something on this Markham story. At least, I think he was. Have you got any idea what it might have been?'

'No idea. Always up to something, old Vernon.' MacLeod's voice softened. 'Listen Nick,' he asked solicitously, '. . . are you all right?'

'Yeah . . . I'm fine.'

'Want to take the day off?'

'No, no . . . I want to work. What've you got?'

'Well,' MacLeod said with false heartiness, 'What do you know about the sexual habits of lions?'

'What?'

'Leonora the lioness,' MacLeod went on with strained jollity. 'The friskiest beast alive. Fucks all day long and then when the Keeper wants to get in to feed her and her feller, she tries to bite his hand off. Apparently she sees him as some sort of sexual threat.'

Mullen made some notes, welcoming the distraction from his thoughts. 'Anything else?' MacLeod handed him a photo of an elderly woman with a bandaged face, bruises and stitches. 'This Violent Britain. Day One. Centre page spread. Mugged by a fourteen-year-old last week. Top it up, Nick. Ring her at home, get a few quotes. She wants to talk. You know the angle. Dear old Edie, everybody's best friend, terrorized by the teeny-bopper louts . . .'

The rest of the day was an unreal blur. 'Leonora the Lioness,' he typed automatically, 'is the Queen of the Jungle in more ways than one. Leonora, one of London Zoo's prized Kenyan big cats, who has already mothered two lions in captivity, is proving more than a handful for her keeper, Terry Benson . . .'

'Night, Nick,' somebody said. He looked up; the news room was practically empty. He looked over

71

at Bayliss's desk again, focusing on something that had been sliding around the edge of his mind all day: the men he had chased into the street the other morning. He had tried to tell Bayliss about it, but . . . there hadn't been time. The fact that it was Bayliss's desk they were trying to break into hadn't seemed particularly significant, but that was before . . . before. Now . . . Mullen waited impatiently for the last reporter to gather up his things and leave. He walked over to Bayliss's desk, sat down in his creaky chair, reached out and touched his old Remington typewriter. Cursing his sentimentality, he tasted tears in his throat. He looked furtively around the empty newsroom and listened for footsteps. Silence. He opened the top drawer.

The contents were predictable: a jumble of expense sheets, stationery, matches, an unopened bottle of vitamin tablets. The next drawer contained much the same sort of thing. The bottom drawer was locked.

Feeling like a criminal, but unable to resist the temptation, he took out his own desk key and tried it in the lock. It went in, but it wouldn't turn. Sitting in Bayliss's chair, he wondered what the dead man would want him to do. In his mind's eye he saw the man Bayliss had called 'our friendly neighbourhood spook.' *What do you stand for, Nick?* His guilt gave way to obsession. Purposefully, he walked out of the newsroom, down the corridor the led to the factory floor. Searching amongst the dark, black, immobile machines, he found the bag in which the printers kept their tools.

Back at Bayliss's desk, Mullen inserted the tip of the crowbar and pushed; the drawer slid open. Again, the contents looked innocuous: a box of tissues, a stapler, pink sheets of old copy, letters, scissors, the usual. On the bottom was a re-cycled, dog-eared foolscap envelope. He carried it back to his own desk and extracted the contents – a small sheaf of papers. Some photocopied pages of Hansard, the verbatim record of Parliamentary debates. Photocopies of articles from the paper, including the MARKHAM PROBES DEATH OF PRISONER story Mullen had found on the photo-copy machine. Three other stories also concerned the escaped prisoner, Steven Dyce – the headlines read HIT AND RUN DRIVER KILLS ESCAPE BOY, CAMPTON BOYS IN ESCAPE DRAMA and ESCAPE BID THAT WENT WRONG. There were copies of TRUDY GETS HER DENNIS story, the LABOUR MPs AT PEACE CONFER-ENCE story and, finally, an article about the bombing of the American embassy in Turkey. Baffled, Mullen turned the envelope upside down over his desk. A microcassette slid out.

Hoping that the tape was the missing link between the apparently unrelated stories, he inserted it into his own micro-recorder. He rewound it, held it close to his ear and pushed the PLAY button. 'Vernon,' an upper class voice said 'it's George.'

'Yes, George,' Bayliss said eagerly. 'Sorry I wasn't in.'

Mullen froze; he heard footsteps approaching. Hastily he switched the recorder off and feigned interest in some papers on his desk. A fellow reporter walked past; 'Forgot my contacts book,' he explained. Interminable minutes later, headed back toward the door.

'Night,' Mullen said casually, his heart racing wildly. 'Have a nice weekend.' Feverishly, sure that he was onto something, he switched the recorder back on. 'Is it safe to talk?' Mullen recognized the voice by the accent and the slight but distinctive stammer.

'Yes,' Bayliss said. 'Go ahead.'

'It's going to be very difficult, Vernon.'

'Well I didn't think it was going to be like walking into Tesco's for a packet of Daz, dear boy.'

'I'm not sure it's possible, that's all.'

'Well, if you managed to clap eyes on the . . .' The man called George interrupted, rendering Bayliss's last word inaudible.

'Clapping eyes on it is one thing, getting a copy out is another.'

'George, it's the Crown Jewels. I can't make anything stand up without it. You've got to try!'

'You do realize, don't you, what the classification of this material is?'

'Yes, dear boy, I do.'

'You're aware that this could mean not just a Section Two charge but a Section One as well . . . You're prepared to take that risk?'

'Yes, George, I know, we're liable to be be-

74

headed in the Tower of London. For God's sake, George, relax! Remember, a journalist, let alone a friend, never reveals a source. You, at least, will be safe. And with a national newspaper behind me, I might stand half a dog's chance. But there will be no cock ups, will there, George? Because you and I are shrewd and intelligent men, are we not?'

'All right, Vernon,' George said, sounding less than completely convinced, 'I'll do what I can.'

Mullen heard the sound of the phone being replaced on the receiver. The rest of the tape was blank.

He put on his raincoat, put the photocopies, cassette and recorder in his pocket, and went home – bereft, perplexed, and determined.

Chapter Eleven

From his bed, Mullen watched dawn light the tall bay windows of the large room that served as bedroom, study and sitting room. He hadn't slept, or even undressed. He'd been playing and rewinding the cassette for hours, straining to make out the crucial word on the tape – the one that explained whatever it was Bayliss's informant had managed to clap his eyes on.

Well, if you managed to clap eyes on the . . .

Clapping eyes on it is one thing, getting a copy out is another . . .

. . . managed to clap eyes on the . .

Clapping eyes on it is one thing, getting a copy out is another . . .

It was hopeless; the word was unintelligible, elusive as the smoke from his cigarette.

He stubbed the cigarette out in the overflowing ashtray, lit another one, and stood up. His body felt bone-weary and battered but his mind was speeding. He stretched, groaned, and reached for the dog-eared envelope he'd found in Bayliss's desk. He spread the photocopied pages out on his own desk and sat down to examine them.

Each one was headed 'Oral Answers' and appeared to cover a different week of Debates, sometimes jumping a number of weeks, between the months of January and May, 1985. In the first one, Dennis Markham was the questioner,

Mr Markham: Would the Minister tell the House whether there is any truth in the reports that have reached me in my constituency that on August 9th of last year a serious accident took place at USAF Brandon involving an aircraft?

Mr Peter Thomson: Mr Speaker, if there were indeed any truth in these reports then I am sure the House would have heard about them long before now. I suggest that the hon. Gentleman pays less heed to the politically motivated rumour-mongering of his friends in the Campaign for Nuclear Disarmament usually intended to undermine confidence in our American allies, and pays more attention to what our enemies are doing.

77

Mr Markham: Does not the hon. Gentleman realize that I have a responsibility to my constituents, in particular those who are living close to one or another of the several American bases in the area and have a genuine fear of such accidents occurring, and therefore have a right to be told about what is going on, not only in their own country but also in their own county?

Mullen skimmed Thomson's rejoinder – standard political rhetoric – and picked up the next page. The names of Mr Dennis Markham and Mr Peter Thomson were there again in bold face, but the Questions and Answers were different.

Mr Markham: Would the Minister tell the House whether or not there is any truth in the more detailed reports that have reached me that on August 9th of last year an F1-11 nuclear capability aircraft crashed when coming in to land at USAF Brandon and, if so, whether the plane in question was carrying nuclear bombs or nuclear missiles?

Mr Peter Thomson: Mr Speaker, I have made exhaustive enquiries into this matter and can confirm to the House that the F1-11 which the hon. Gentleman refers to suffered a landing equipment fault and crashed into some outbuildings on the base. There was no loss of life and some limited damage to the aircraft and outbuildings. While I can neither confirm nor deny whether the aircraft in question was carrying nuclear weaponry, since this is an operational matter, and is not in the national interest to reveal, I can however assure the hon. Gentleman that precautions on NATO bases against possible nuclear accidents are virtually fail-safe.

Mullen turned to the next page; Markham was again asking the questions, but this time of a different Minister, and on a completely different subject.

Mr Markham: Would the Minister tell the House that he is completely satisfied with the verdict of the inquest on Steven Dyce at the Thetford Coroner's

Court on October 9th of last year? Can the Minister assure us that all the significant and substantial evidence regarding Steven Dyce's death was submitted to the Coroner?

Mr Anthony Walker-Smith: Mr Speaker: I can assure the House that this matter has been thoroughly investigated. A most able police officer of Superintendent rank . . .

Mullen began skimming again: ' . . . team investigated this matter for months . . . statements . . . parents . . . were taken down.' He picked up the photocopied *Dispatch* article headed HIT AND RUN DRIVER KILLS ESCAPE BOY.

The inquest was heard yesterday at Thetford Coroner's Court on Steven Anthony Dyce of Netherton Estate, London. Steven, who had escaped from a work party at Campton Youth Custody Centre in Norfolk on August 9th, was found dead on August 11th on the outskirts of Thetford. The pathologist indicated that the time of death was 36 hours before the discovery of the body, and that the cause of death was a hit-and-run driver.

The final article had appeared in a provincial paper, the *Eastern Daily Press*; headed CAMPTON BOYS IN ESCAPE DRAMA, it was dated August 10th, 1984.

Police yesterday were still hunting two Borstal

boys who made a sensational escape from high-security Campton Youth Custody Centre. Steven Dyce, 17, and Michael Parker, 17, both of London, are the first detainees to escape from Campton in over five years. A spokesman said yesterday that full enquiry would be made into security at the Centre.

Mullen began making notes. 'Questions in House – insubstantial evidence regarding hit-and-run death. Escaped August 9th, Found August 11th. *Two* boys in escape.' Why the discrepancies, he wondered, in what seemed, on the face of it, a simple, straightforward event. Why was the name of Michael Parker missing from all but the initial account of the escape? Why had it taken 36 hours to discover Dyce's body? And what lay behind Markham's interest in Dyce? Certainly there was nothing here relating to Markham's connection with Kleist. Had his desire to prove his old friend's innocence impaired Vernon's judgment? The contents of the envelope proved nothing – nothing at all. If only he could read the dead man's mind . . .

What was the significance of August 9th? The escape . . . the alleged accident . . . the escape. He read through the CAMPTON BOYS IN ESCAPE DRAMA again, looking between the lines for a lead. It was there, all right – so obvious that he'd almost missed it. The byline. He reached for the phone.

The *Eastern Daily Press* was an evening paper; Roger Messiter was already at work. 'Just hold on while I dig out my old notebook,' Messiter said, happy to help a fellow reporter.

'I'd be very grateful,' said Mullen, trying to keep a lid on his impatience. He lit another cigarette and doodled on his notepad.

'Here it is,' Messiter said at last. 'Dyce and Parker were definitely on that escape together.'

'What about the inquest – was Parker there?'

'Hang on . . . No. He wasn't there. The only witnesses were the local copper investigating the hit-and-run and the police doctor.'

'Are you sure?'

'Positive.'

'Right. Look, I need to talk to Dyce's mum and dad.'

'Got a pen?'

The address Messiter gave him was Netherton Estates, a bleak wasteland in northeast London. The whole place looked deserted; if it hadn't already been condemned, Mullen thought, it deserved to be. The door with the number Roger had given him was at the end of a dark narrow corridor, littered with rubbish and stinking of urine. It was boarded up – with graffiti-covered chipboard. He would have to contact Challis.

Fred Challis was one of the few people in the world Mullen disliked more than Harry Champion. Challis was a necessary evil in the reporter's life – a cop who, for a usurious price, provided information unobtainable through regular official channels. Mullen arranged to meet him at the usual place on a seedy run down street in Hoxton; he waited in the doorway of a boarded-up shop, seeking shelter from the downpour, stamping his feet to keep them warm. A car parked some thirty yards away, dipped its lights, then turned them off altogether.

'Sadistic bastard,' Mullen thought, running through the deluge. The driver, a slightly simian, middle-aged man with a cigar planted firmly in his mouth, leaned over to unlock the back door – taking his time, Mullen noted with annoyance. Mullen got into the back seat and sat tensely as Challis drove slowly, aimlessly, along the rain-slick streets. The police radio crackled; Challis reached for the microphone on the dashboard and spoke into it. 'Oscar Tango – one-seven to HQ.'

'Yes, one-seven?' came the answer from head-quarters.

'D.S. Challis, CRO inquiry . . . '

'Go ahead, one-seven . . . '

'Suspect named Michael Parker . . . No middle names known. Believed resident London. No other information available. Require present where-abouts.'

Challis replaced the microphone and waited for an answer. 'You don't half try it on, Mullen,' he said.

The radio crackled back into life. 'Oscar Tango, one-seven?'

'Yeah,' Challis said into the mike, 'go ahead HQ.'

'Michael James Parker. CRO file 121348 stroke 84. Born 2.2.67 . . . address, 91 Kitchener Court, Dalston Lane, E8.'

'Is that his present whereabouts, HQ?'

'Hang on a sec, one-seven . . . No. His present whereabouts is Greenmont Remand Centre.'

'Can you confirm that, HQ?'

'Yes, one-seven. Present whereabouts Greenmont Remand Centre. Thank you, HQ. Over.' Challis clipped the mike back on the dash.

'Damn!' said Mullen. 'How the hell am I going to get in there?'

'No chance, mate, they don't exactly welcome reporters with open arms, y'know.' Challis pulled the car into an alleyway and stopped. Disappointed, disgusted, miserably cold and wet, Mullen opened the door. 'Oi!' the cop said sharply. He held his right hand over his shoulder snapping his fingers in a gesture Mullen knew well. Wordlessly, Mullen took an envelope from his coat pocket and handed it over – Challis's fee for services rendered. Challis shot him a thoroughly unpleasant smile and drove away.

Mullen moved into another doorway to consider his next move. Shivering, he consulted his dilapidated A to Z. E8 . . . Dalston Lane . . .

Chapter Twelve

The Dalston council flats didn't look any more habitable than the abandoned estate where Mullen had looked for Dyce's family – the same graffiti-splattered walls, the same boarded-up windows and doors. There were children around, though; several of them followed him, as though he was the Pied Piper, to what he hoped was the Parkers' door.

The woman who answered was the colour of an old sheet, yellowed after many washings. 'Mrs Parker?' she nodded. 'My name's Nick Mullen. I'm a reporter. I'd like to talk to you about your son.'

'Which one?' Her faded blue eyes regarded him with suspicion.

'Michael. You see, I need some information . . . May I come in?' Not waiting for an invitation, he walked past her into a small room that smelled of damp, and of rancid grease. Three children picked their noses and watched thè television set.

'What's he gone and done now?' the woman asked in a whiny voice.

'Who?'

'Micky.'

'No, no . . . he hasn't done anything. It's a friend of his, Steven Dyce, that I need to know about.' On the gas ring, a kettle was boiling; the woman reached for a tea bag and motioned for Mullen to sit down at the table. 'Thanks.' She handed him a cup of weak tea and a stale biscuit. 'The thing is, Mrs Parker, when your son broke out of the detention centre last August, he wasn't alone. The boy he was with was killed, you know.'

'No,' she said with evident surprise. 'I didn't know nothing about that. What happened?'

'That's what I'm trying to find out,' Mullen explained. 'I'm actually looking for the family of the other boy, you see – Steven Dyce.'

'I'm sorry,' she said apologetically, 'but I just don't have no recollection of nobody of that name. Micky's friends all seemed the same to me – a bad lot. Not that Micky's any angel, you understand, but he never got into no serious trouble till he started hanging out with them punks. Sniffin' glue and stealin' cars, that was all they ever thought about. No, I can't remember no Steven. But then, I have trouble remembering the name of the Prime Minister, know what I mean?'

Mullen poured some evaporated milk into his tea and stirred it. 'When was the last time you saw your son, Mrs Parker?'

The woman looked guiltily down at the table.

'Not for a while. It's hard for me to get down there, see. I haven't been well . . . and there are the children to look after . . . '

'I understand,' Mullen said sympathetically. 'It's hard . . . '

'Micky's a good boy!' she said insistently. 'It's just that . . . see, I was only thirteen when Micky was born.' That made her younger than he was, Mullen realized with a shock; she looked as old as his mother. 'What did I know about raising a kid?' she went on. 'I was just a babe myself. I did my best, but . . . '

'I'm sure you did, Mrs Parker I'm sure you did. Look,' Mullen said, glancing at his watch. 'If I could just talk to Micky . . . '

'How you going to do that? It ain't up to me, y'know.'

'If you could just give me the name of a relative . . . '

'Plenty of those,' she said.

'Who?'

'There's my brother Clifford . . . ' The front door opened and a burly man lurched into the room, smelling like a brewery. He peered blearily at Mullen. 'Who's he?' he asked the woman.

'A reporter.'

'What's he doing here?' he asked, belligerently.

'I'm just leaving,' Mullen said hurriedly.

'What the bloody hell's he doing here?' the man shouted.

'Clifford Parker?' Mullen asked, halfway through the door.

'Harris.'
'Thanks.'

The Visitors' Waiting Room at the Greenmont
Remand Centre reminded Mullen of a smaller
version of a Social Security Office, only worse:
cold, institutional, oppressive. 'Trainees L to R,' a
guard announced. With a score of other visitors,
Mullen stood up and followed the guard to a barred
gate. They waited while the guard unlocked it, then
waited again for the arrival of a second guard, who
led them down a corridor with a steel door at the
end of it. The second guard rang a bell and a small
hatch in the door was opened from the other side.
A third guard unlocked the door, which Mullen
noticed was several inches thick. If Campton was
anything like this, he thought, Dyce and Parker
must have been fairly bright to have escaped.

With the other visitors, he was herded through a
landing overlooking a hall in which long tables
were set up in neat rows. The E to K 'Trainees' sat
on one side, their visitors on the other. Each visitor
had to check in with the guard at the desk on the
landing. Standing in the queue, Mullen couldn't
help feeling intimidated; he wondered whether he
looked as nervous as he felt. If so, he thought,
they'd surely arrest him.

He watched as the E to K people were ushered
out and the L to R trainees led in. In front of him,
visitors matter-of-factly signed their names.
'Visiting Order?' the guard asked him. Sweating

profusely, thinking that he'd make a lousy spy, Mullen held out a slip of paper. The guard looked at it, wrote something in the book and turned it around for him to sign. With a hand that shook only slightly, he wrote, 'Clifford Harris.'

Downstairs, he was escorted through the vast room, hazy with cigarette smoke, past rows of people discussing some of the most intimate details of their lives amidst this noisy crowd of strangers. Some argued, some wept; most showed no emotion at all, merely trying to stay afloat in the sewer of the system. Hawk-eyed guards walked up and down the aisles and stood against the walls.

Mullen had been worried about how he would recognize Micky Parker, but he needn't have been concerned; the guard led him directly to a chair opposite a skinny boy with stringy blond hair, surly blue eyes and a spotty complexion that seemed never to have been touched by the sun. 'Don't say a word,' Mullen whispered as he sat down.

'But you're not . . . !' Parker blurted out.

'*Don't say a word*,' Mullen hissed. 'I know I'm not your uncle Clifford. Your mum sorted it out for me, okay? It was the only way I could get to see you.' Parker got the message; he nodded shrewdly. 'My name's Nick Mullen. I'm a re-porter.'

The boy ignored Mullen's outstretched hand. He leaned back, sizing the stranger up. 'You gonna tell me I've won a million quid on the bingo?'

Mullen leaned forward and kept his voice low. 'I'm trying to find out about Steven Dyce.'

'Dicey?' Parker asked, smirking. 'What's he gone and done now? Robbed a bank?'

Mullen was taken aback; he hesitated. How could the boy think that Dyce was alive? Surely he'd been with him when . . . '

'What's happened?' Parker asked, sensing something wrong.

'You haven't heard, then?'

'Heard *what*, for fuck's sake?'

'Steven's dead.'

'Fuck off,' the boy shouted. What kind of trick was this bloke trying to play on him? The nearest guard watched them like a hawk. Stay calm, Mullen told himself, or you'll blow it. He reached into his pocket for the photocopied article about the inquest and handed it to Parker. 'A hit-and-run accident,' he said. 'It's all in there.'

Parker studied the article and exploded again. 'The rotten, lying bastards! They told me he was still on the run! I thought he was shacked up with some bird!'

Fearing that anything he said might excite the boy more, Mullen kept quiet. He moved his coat from his lap to the table in front of him and surreptitiously switched on the microcassette recorder underneath it. In a few moments, Parker looked calmer. 'I'm sorry,' Mullen said, handing him a cigarette. 'I thought you knew.' Parker looked ill, as though he'd been kicked in the stomach. 'Will you tell me about the escape?'

Parker took a long drag on his cigarette. 'What escape? I'm still inside, ain't I?' Mullen waited, hoping that the boy's need to talk would overcome his resentment. The cassette turned, dutifully recording coughs, chairs scraping, overlapping fragments of other people's conversations. His defences momentarily down, Parker relaxed and relented slightly. 'We nicked a motor in Thetford, right, and then about fifteen minutes later, the Old Bill caught up with us. So we pulled up and done a runner. Only I weren't quick enough out, and they nicked me.'

'What about Steve?'

'He climbed over a fence! He got away! That was the last time I saw him.' Parker stared at the article in front of him, turning something over in his mind. 'Funny how they found him the same day I was ghosted.'

'What?'

Parker looked furtively round at the guard. 'Back at the nick, I get twenty-one days Chokey, right? I've done two days of me Chokey when all of a sudden they ghost me . . . Moved me out that nick up in East Anglia and shunt me down here. In the middle of the night. Ghost Trained.' Puzzled, he took another long drag. 'Another thing . . . it says here he was found on the morning of the eleventh, but the pa . . path . . . '

'Pathologist.'

'Yeah, him. He reckons the time of death was thirty-six hours before. Well, you work it out. Twenty-four hours before is the tenth, right?'

Mullen did some mental arithmetic. 'Thirty-six hours before is the ninth – the night of the ninth.'

'Which is when Old Bill stopped us.'

'I think you've got something there, Micky.' Mullen thought for a moment, then snapped his fingers triumphantly. 'You should have been at the Inquest . . . because you were the last person to see him alive.'

'Me and the two coppers who caught me.'

'No belongings on the table, sir.' The guard was standing directly behind Mullen; startled, he moved his coat – and recorder – back into his lap. The guard moved away.

'Why didn't they want you as a witness, then?' Mullen asked. Parker looked blank. 'Maybe you saw something you weren't supposed to see.'

'Like what? It was pitch dark.' Mullen noticed that some of the 'trainees' were being herded out of the room. 'You said Steve climbed over a fence,' he said urgently. 'Do you know what was on the other side?'

'Dunno . . . everything happened so quick. All I remember is that one minute I was in a nice Ford Sierra, the next I was banged up in the back of a police car.'

'Do you know where it was?' Parker shook his head. 'Come on, Micky,' Mullen insisted. 'You've *got* to remember!'

'It was south of Thetford. On some poxy side road. It was massive. Round a building site, it was.'

'Time's up,' the guard said. Parker stood up and began moving toward the door, the guard right behind him.

'Do me a favour, right?' he called over his shoulder. 'Get my mum to write to me.' He stood in the doorway, the guard frisking him for contraband. 'Don't forget.'

Chapter Thirteen

Back at his flat, Mullen spread a road map out on his desk and examined the Norfolk area like a cryptogram. 'South of Thetford,' Parker had said. Thetford meant nothing to Mullen; he'd never been near it. Suddenly there it was, blazing at him like a neon sign – not the town, but the small black symbol just below it. An airbase.

Mullen tried to keep a lid on his rising excitement; he'd been on too many wild goose chases to get carried away. The logical thing would be to have an early night and drive up to Norfolk in the morning. Since he didn't really know what he was looking for, he could at least look for it in daylight. Even as he gave himself that sensible advice, he was reaching for his coat.

Driving into the bitter fen wind that blew across the flat, depressing Norfolk landscape, Mullen knew why he'd never been there before; surely no one would go there if they could help it. Through the gathering dusk he could see, in every direction, tedious vistas of nothingness. He saw the faint, pinkish glow of lights in the distance. As he got closer, he made them out to be long, parallel rows of runway lights.

He turned off the main road onto the narrower public road that encircled the air base. Driving slowly, parallel to a high wire fence, he saw a guard house, a plane taxiing, another being refuelled. A Range Rover passed him, driving in the opposite direction. Could this be the road on which Steven Dyce was killed? Behind him, another car approached, flashed its headlights, and hooted and overtook him; a man in an American airman's uniform leaned out the window and yelled something at him as it passed. If this *was* the road, how could a body have lain undiscovered on it for a day and a half?

Inside the fence, military vehicles moved, ghost-like, through the darkness – phantoms of war. A sign read CONTRACTOR'S TRAFFIC STRAIGHT ON and, below that, the name and logo of the contractor, Crozier Brown. Someone had almost obscured the words with black, spray-painted graffiti. Mullen made out the words DEATH CAMP and a CND symbol. He drove on.

He passed the main gate, where floodlights illuminated a guard post surrounded by sandbags. Guards – some of them, he noticed with surprise, female – checked the vehicles passing into and out of the security area. A few hundred yards later, the opposite side of the road opened out into a large, brightly-lit car park. There, in the nothingness of Norfolk, Mullen found himself staring at Middle America – a brightly-lit supermarket, barber shop and hamburger joint. A building slightly separate from the rest had a sign over its door reading 'The Panhandle Club' and, next to it, a neon Budwieser sign. Three men out of uniform but with unmistakable military haircuts entered the club and were checked in at the door.

A brown Cortina drove into the car park; Mullen noticed it because every other car, except his own BMW, was American. He drove slowly back out into the road that followed the perimeter fence. Behind him, Middle America vanished like a mirage. Ahead, the darkness of the outer reaches of the airfield was broken occasionally by distant points of light. When the road forked, he turned left in the direction that followed the fence – a country lane that ended abruptly at a set of gates. He switched off his headlights and stopped the car.

The noise of the plane that had just taken off receded; only the sound of the wind broke the silence of the country night. Mullen gazed through the windscreen at the gates – about ten feet high, topped with huge rolls of barbed wire. Additional rolls of barbed wire lay on the ground near a small, apparently unmanned guard post. A cluster of hangars, surrounded by pools of light, stood inside a second security fence perhaps two hundred yards away. Beyond them were the pink, misty lights of the runway.

He climbed over a fence, Parker had said. *He got away*. Mullen got out of the car and walked to the gates. A sign posted inside read

THIS IS A PROHIBITED PLACE WITHIN THE MEANING OF THE OFFICIAL SECRETS ACT. UNAUTHORIZED PERSONS MAY BE ARRESTED AND PROSECUTED.

He looked up at the fence; it would have been a difficult, if not impossible, climb. Hearing a car approach, he turned, squinting in the glare of its headlights. He stood his ground, motionless, as the blue-and-white police car, its occupants staring hard at him, slid past and disappeared into the night.

Heedless of the cold, he peered through the fence, his face almost touching the wire mesh. A mongrel dog trotted up and sniffed his feet. He heard the whine of an aircraft engine starting up and watched as the grey, streamlined profile of an F1-11 aircraft backed slowly, menacingly, out of one of the hangars and stopped in a pool of light. Vehicles moved round it, soldier ants servicing their queen. The dog began to bark. He spun around, nearly jumping out of his skin: someone just inches away had switched on a torch and was shining it in his face.

'Before they put that barbed wire up,' a female voice said brightly, 'we used to get in all the time by this gate. It's still a cinch with a good pair of wire cutters.' He grabbed for the torch; she relinquished it, unresisting, and he pointed it in her direction. She wore jeans, boots and a donkey

97

jacket, and looked about sixteen. What the hell was *she* doing here, he wondered.

'Look!' she said proudly, retrieving her torch and pointing it at a concrete bunker about fifty yards inside the fence. 'That's us!' Mullen could just make out the CND peace symbol and the word, PEACE. She grinned, 'What are you then, a Russian spy?'

'Reporter,' Mullen said, recovering his equilibrium. 'When did you say they put the barbed wire up?'

'After the accident.'

'What accident?'

'One of their stupid little planes crashed. You should have seen it – smoke and flames everywhere. Scared us all shitless.' In the distance, a car sounded its hooter. 'That's me dad,' the girl said cheerfully. 'I've gotta go. Bye . . . '

As suddenly as she'd appeared, she was gone, the dog scampering after her. Mullen heard a car door slam. The car drove away. He turned back to the fence, transfixed. The F1-11 was still there, surrounded by vehicles and personnel. Bomb-shaped objects – missiles? – were being attached to each wing of the plane.

The Thetford Public Library was closing, but Mullen, using all his charm, wheedled the librarian into giving him 'just five more minutes.' He was almost ready to give up, anyway; his search of back issues of the local weekly, *The Thetford and*

Watton Times, had yielded nothing more than the usual trivia: births, marriages, deaths, football games, farming news, garden parties and petty crimes. Only one story had anything at all to do with the military installation, and it told of a local man who had sneaked in on a bet.

Mullen was a sceptic, but he had no use for people who believed that governments spent all their time plotting sinister conspiracies. Still, if Steven Dyce *had* managed to climb over the fence onto the base, why all the secrecy? It would have been embarrassing, but no more so than the story about the man who'd won his bet. What exactly had happened on the night of August 9th that had made Dyce's presence such a threat? What had Markham been sniffing around with his questions about an accident? Had he found any answers? If he had, Mullen knew it was bloody unlikely that he'd tell him – not after the story he'd done on Trudy Markham. *One of their silly little planes crashed.* Had the girl been talking about the same accident? All his instincts told him something was being covered up, but ambiguity and innuendo weren't enough; he needed hard evidence.

Mullen yawned; he was hungry and tired, his eyes were burning, and the librarian was frowning at him wanting to lock up, and there it was:

MYSTERY EVACUATION FROM BASE
IS JUST EXERCISE

Villagers living in Brandon were alarmed last Thursday when a 'steady convoy' of vehicles from the nearby American base poured through the village centre late at night, the sound awakening them in their beds. 'The cars were full of women and children,' said villager, John Rivett.

A spokesman from the United States Air Force said there had been no reason for any alarm, as they had been engaged in an exercise to check emergency procedures. He regretted any distress caused to the villagers of Brandon.

The paper was dated August 16, 1984. Jolted wide awake, Mullen fumbled in his attaché case for his desk diary. August 16th of last year had been a Thursday. 'Last Thursday' had been August 9th.

Chapter Fourteen

In the grey light of the following afternoon, the base looked quite different from the night before – prosaic and relatively harmless. With the planes out of sight, presumably housed in their hangars, the menace of the night before was missing.

The young woman in an American air force blue uniform who leaned out the window hatch in the guard house at the main gate looked as innocuous, Mullen thought, as an air hostess. 'Good afternoon,' he said, smiling. 'I have an appointment with Lieutenant Colonel Lehane for four-thirty.'

'And your name is, sir?'

'Mr Mullen.'

The guard consulted a book, her eyes slowly following her finger down the list of names. Mullen turned off his motor and lit a cigarette. Eventually, the guard picked up her telephone and dialled. 'Hi, Sandra. I have Mr Mullen here for four-thirty.' She put the phone down and handed Mullen a clipboard with a form on which he was to fill in his name, time of arrival, person visited, car registration and signature. He did so, handed it back, and waited while she checked the information. With a plastic smile, she handed him a plastic badge that said VISITOR PASS. 'There you go,' she said. 'Colonel Lehane's office is upstairs in the administration building, over there.' She pointed to a two-story structure near the control tower. 'Have a nice day!'

Feeling that he'd just entered a foreign country, and under somewhat false pretences, Mullen parked beside the drab, boxlike building. A sign by the entrance said

THE MISSION OF THE 20TH TACTICAL FIGHTER WING IN PEACE IS TO PREPARE FOR WAR. DON'T YOU FORGET IT!

Lieutenant-Colonel Walter S. Lehane was a greying, paunchy man in his late forties with a jovial manner. Disarmament was his style, if not his government's. As Commander of Public Affairs, Lehane was responsible for maintaining friendly relations with the community; he knew better than to keep the press waiting. He greeted Mullen in his outer office, shaking hands as warmly as though the meeting had been his idea. His secretary asked Mullen how he took his coffee and hastened to make it, while Lehane ushered him down a corridor lined with framed photographs: Lehane on a podium, delivering a speech; a Cruise missile, sailing through an azure sky, for all the world like a Pan AM clipper en route to some idyllic holiday destination; a group of children posed around an F1-11 on the tarmac. 'That one's my favourite,' Lehane said, in a soft Southern drawl. 'The local primary school. The boys wanted to be shown around the place, so we laid it on for them.'

Lehane's inner sanctum contained more photos, plaques and assorted Americana. Another picture of a Cruise missile, this one poster-size, with the legend 'CRUISE MISSILES: A Vital Part of the West's Life Insurance.' In a photo of a soccer team, two uniformed Air Forcemen propped up each side of the Eleven like bookends. 'Those guys are third in the league,' Lehane said, tapping the photo with his forefinger.

'Only third?' Mullen said with a smile.

'Well,' said the Colonel, chuckling. 'You show me a bunch of English boys who can do as well at American football.'

The secretary brought Mullen his coffee. 'Please sit down, Mr Mullen,' Lehane said expansively, taking a seat behind a desk the size of a small runway. Reagan and Thatcher looked down from their photos on the wall behind Lehane – Reagan smiling, Thatcher stern. An American flag hung in one corner of the room, the Union Jack in another. 'We've been here for over thirty years, you know. That's a hell of a long time. You start to form ties, friendships. The local people – the natives, I mean – ' Lehane smiled at his own mistake, 'get kinda used to having you around.'

'You're not trying to tell me you don't have any

problems, surely,' Mullen said, sounding as genial as Lehane.

Lehane chuckled. 'That's all you guys are ever interested in. You never want to hear about the good stuff.' He leaned back in his chair, a practised veteran of dozens of interviews with smartass journalists like this one. 'Okay. What sort of problems did you have in mind?'

'Well,' Mullen said, handing Lehane a photocopy of the article headed MYSTERY EVACUATION FROM BASE, 'I'm very curious about something I read in the local paper.' Lehane scanned it quickly; it was clearly very familiar to him. He handed it back to Mullen with a look of undisguised contempt. 'I wondered if you had any further comment on it, Colonel?'

'No, I don't,' Lehane said, still courteous, but cooling. 'It's all in the article.'

'An exercise?'

'That's right.'

'What was the purpose of the exercise?'

'We are a United States Air Force Main Operating Base. In the event of an outbreak of hostilities, we're a primary target. Personnel and their families have to be one hundred per cent prepared for such an eventuality. We've had twenty, maybe thirty, Survival Response exercises in this area in the last ten years. Now, all of a sudden some wiseguy local reporter thinks he's got the makings of a good story. Take my word for it, Mr Mullen, the story's a non-starter.'

Mullen looked genuinely puzzled. 'Then how

104

would you account for the fact that according to this article, the women and children seemed in a state of panic?'

Lehane regarded him steadily. 'Well, to tell you the truth, Mr Mullen, I've never understood that myself. If, as the article states, the convoy was proceeding at seventy miles per hour through Brandon, it'd be mighty hard to see what kind of mood anyone was in – unless, of course, you happened to be running alongside. And as the man who's quoted is sixty-five years of age, I don't see that as a feasible proposition.'

Mullen studied the article. 'It also says here that a panic-stricken Air Force man was seen to hail a taxi outside the base's main gate saying, Go anywhere, just get the hell out of here.'

'Well,' Lehane said dismissively, 'we've never been able to ascertain who the officer alleged to have said that is, so it's impossible for me to comment. Frankly, I think it's a lot of baloney.' Mullen looked half-convinced. 'Are there any other "problems" I can help you with?'

'Yes,' Mullen said. 'As a matter of fact, there is one other thing.' Lehane waited for the zinger these reporters always threw at you when they thought your guard was down. 'What would happen if – hypothetically – I were to climb over your fence and get into the base?'

Lehane didn't hesitate: 'You'd be detected and apprehended within minutes.'

'There's no way I could escape detection?'

'Absolutely not.'

105

'And no way I could escape apprehension?'

'No way.'

'Would there be any chance of my getting shot, Colonel?'

'Sure there would be,' Lehane answered. 'What do you think we're going to do? Say, Go ahead, steal a nuclear warhead? All security personnel are instructed to fire at the legs after two warnings to stop. Fortunately, we've never had the occasion to do that.'

Mullen leaned forward, abandoning all pretence. 'Supposing I got killed accidentally?'

Lehane snorted dismissively. 'You sure do like problems, don't you, Mr Mullen? You can't expect me to comment on a hypothesis like that.'

'What if I were a borstal boy?'

'Pardon me?'

'What if I were a borstal boy?'

'If you were a borstal boy, you would be under lock and key.'

'I'm not. I'm on the run.'

Lehane wasn't easily fazed; he took his time. 'Okay, Mr Mullen – what's the beef?'

Mullen paused, then took the plunge. 'I have information that a young man by the name of Steven Dyce climbed into the base while on the run from the local Borstal. Do you have a comment on that, Colonel?'

'Well, I certainly don't have any knowledge of it,' Lehane said, 'but I'd be happy to have it checked out for you and let you know.'

'I certainly hope you can, Colonel, because that

appears to be the last time he was seen alive.'

'Well, that's a very serious allegation, Mr Mullen. But don't you think,' Lehane said smoothly, 'that if something as serious as that had happened, you would have heard about it a long time ago?' He rose, signifying that the interview was over. The two men exchanged a look of perfect understanding.

'Have a good day now, y'hear?' the guard called after Mullen as he drove past the guard house and out the gate.

Chapter Fifteen

Mullen was pensive as he drove back to London on the motorway. He passed a road sign that said LONDON 45 and glanced from it to his rear view mirror, which reflected the lights of the car behind him. He mentally reviewed what he knew about Steven Dyce's death. The date. The road. The fence. The 'accident'. If the timing of the evacuation of the base had been a coincidence, it strained credibility. Still, stranger things had happened. Considering the implications of his suspicions, he wanted to believe Colonel Lehane. But one thing Bayliss had taught him – had hammered at him time and again during countless late night discussions of their profession – was to trust his instincts. His instincts told him Lehane was lying.

He probably knew as much now, he reckoned, as Markham did – but like Markham, he still hadn't anything solid enough to go public. He reached into his pocket for a cigarette, only to realize that he was already holding a lighted one in his other hand. His body was screaming for sleep. Driving through an illuminated section of road, he glanced again into the rear view mirror; was the car behind him the same brown Cortina he'd seen in the parking lot at the base the day before, or was fatigue clouding his judgment, causing him to think he was being followed? He increased his speed, swung out and overtook the car ahead. In his side view mirror, he saw the Cortina do the same.

Spotting a lay-by just ahead, he slowed, flashed his indicator light and pulled over. The Cortina whistled past. Greatly relieved, and feeling slightly foolish, he drove back onto the road. Incipient paranoia, he told himself; better watch it.

He reached the outskirts of London when suddenly he remembered something that snapped him wide awake. In his obsession with Steven Dyce, he had paid almost no attention to another of the stories Bayliss had photocopied. It had seemed so unrelated to the Dyce affair that he had passed it by for what seemed a fresher scent. Where had he left it? At home, on his desk?

He had. He found it buried under the Hansards records, the pile of cuttings about the Dyce escape and the inquest, and the microtape of George's cryptic phone call. It was a front-page story from *The Times*: U.S. EMBASSY IN ANKARA BOMBED. MANY FEARED DEAD. He read it rapidly, then read the final paragraph again. 'A Pentagon spokesman said that all United States air, ground and sea forces had been placed on full alert.' The story had run on August 10th, 1984.

He picked up the phone, dialled the overseas operator and jotted down the numbers he was given. Take it slow, he told himself – blow this phone call and you might not get another chance. He stood up, lit a cigarette and put Schubert's String Quintet on his record player, hoping to soothe his jagged nerves. It didn't help.

The flat looked like a tip, he thought. He washed some cups, hung up some clothes, organized his laundry and threw out some food that was rotting in the fridge. He made a pot of coffee. Finally, with great deliberation, he opened his attaché case, took out his microcassette recorder and inserted a blank tape. He attached the telephone lead and fitted the little rubber suction device to the receiver. He did a voice test to make sure the machine was recording. Then he dialled the fourteen digits he'd written down and waited, doodling little missiles on his notepad, for the Pentagon to answer its phone.

'Press Office, please,' he told the switchboard operator.

'Army, Navy or Air Force?'

'Air Force.'

'Hold on, please.' Another phone rang, another voice answered. 'Quinlan.' He sounded confident, authoritative, official.

'Good afternoon,' Mullen said, awkwardly trying – he wasn't sure why – to disguise his voice. 'It is afternoon in Washington, isn't it? My name is

Gordon Carey. I'm writing a piece on the F1-11 for *War Monthly* here in London. I wonder if you could help me.'

'That's what we're here for, Mr Carey.'

'Good.' Mullen tried to sound as businesslike as the voice on the other end. 'First of all, would I be correct in saying that F1-11 aircraft stationed at the main United States operating bases in the UK are on continuous alert?'

'QRA or Quick Reflex Alert. Yes, you would be correct Mr Carey.'

'Does that mean that the aircraft are armed with nuclear weapons?'

'Yes,' Quinlan's hesitation was barely perceptible, but Mullen imagined he heard tumblers clicking into place in the official's head. 'I'm sorry?' he said, wanting to make sure that the tape picked up Quinlan's words.

'Yes,' Quinlan repeated uneasily. 'I said it does.'

'Can you tell me under what circumstances Quick Reflex Alert aircraft might go on a flying mission?'

'I would have thought that was self-evident, Mr Carey.' Quinlan sounded wary now, getting a whiff of something not quite right in the air.

'An alert?'

'Yes.'

'I wonder if you could tell me what would happen,' Mullen asked, choosing his words carefully, 'if – hypothetically – a QRA aircraft were to crash with its nuclear payload still on board.'

Without warning, the line went dead. 'Hello?

. . . Hello?' Mullen put the phone down, bewildered; then picked it up again, heard a dialling tone and redialled the number. He heard the series of hollow clicks that normally accompany trans-atlantic calls – but the next sound made him recoil with shock. Instead of the expected ring, the sound of his own voice came through the receiver, eerily echoing his last question to Quinlan. He replaced the receiver and stared at it. There was only one explanation. He wasn't the only one who had recorded the conversation.

Sitting at his desk in the brightly-lit room, he felt frozen with fear. He remembered Bayliss's boozy references to 'our friendly neighbourhood spook.' He had never felt so vulnerable, or so frightened. He turned out the lights and stood at the window, his eyes searching the empty street and dark windows of the flat across the road. Slowly, he lowered his blinds.

Switching on his desk light, he surveyed the room, considering possible hiding places, all of which seemed laughably obvious. He hurried into the kitchen and examined the contents of his cupboards. He opened the fridge. Some eggs. Five cans of McEwans. A carton of orange juice.

He removed the carton of orange juice, poured the contents into the sink and rinsed it with water from the tap. Rummaging in a drawer he found a polythene bag. Back at his desk, he rolled up the papers he'd found in Bayliss's desk and wrapped them, and the microcassette, in the polythene bag. He stuffed it all into the orange juice carton and

112

replaced it in the fridge. He peered out the kitchen window, checking the street again, and the building across the way. The street and the building looked deserted; but if he'd been stark naked, he couldn't have felt more exposed.

Chapter Sixteen

MacLeod studied Mullen's bloodshot eyes, unshaven chin and dishevelled clothing. The reporter looked like hell, he thought. Smelled a bit ripe, as well. 'Okay,' he sighed, riffling through the pages of rough copy Mullen had been up all night typing, 'Let's go over this again. There's a bad crash on a U.S. air base. Markham gets wind of what's going on and starts asking a lot of awkward questions in the House, but is fobbed off with political double talk. When he starts to make the connection between the discrepancies in the Dyce Inquest and the aircraft accident, the government, or persons unknown in the government, decide to play dirty and plant a story that discredits Markham totally and finishes him as a credible political force, which they do. And the whole thing would have been forgotten – '

'Covered up.'

'If it weren't for Vernon and some Deep Throat character who either did or did not give Vernon some document, some file, that somebody did or did not steal when they broke into his flat. How's that for a precis? Have I got it right?'

'That's good, Jack.'

'What have you been taking, magic mushrooms?' Mullen's eyes flashed with anger. 'The whole thing's fucking paranoid fantasy, Nick! You know what it sounds like? It sounds like any one of those cock-and-bull conspiracy stories about the Kennedy assassination and the CIA!'

'Jack,' Mullen said agitatedly, rising halfway out of his chair, 'I'm telling you, there was a bad crash on that base last year!'

'Okay, okay – I'll go along with that. No problem. You say your research is solid, so, okay, yes, I'm prepared to believe there was a crash involving an F1-11 nuclear capability bomber last year – '

'And that it was serious – very serious?'

'Maybe. I'm also prepared to believe that the Ministry didn't want it to get out. We know what they're capable of – the Falklands business showed that – and I'm even prepared to believe there might, there just *might* have been some funny business at the Inquest – '

'So give me the story, Jack!'

'*But* . . . as for Members of Parliament being framed because of their opposition to some government line – Jesus Christ, Nick, you really ought to know better. It just won't stand up. And for one very good reason – Kleist, the KGB man. Where does he fit into all this, eh? How d'you get

115

a known KGB man to help you frame an anti-NATO British MP?'

'Well,' said Mullen, sinking back into his chair, 'I agree that Kleist is a stumbling block.'

'A stumbling block?? It's a bloody ten foot reinforced concrete wall, you daft twit!'

'So give me the airbase part of the story, Jack.'

'What?'

'You said you could go along with that part of it okay? So put your money where your mouth is. Let me try and find out more about what really happened on the ninth – whether the Inquest really was fiddled.'

'No,' MacLeod said firmly, handing Nick his pages of copy.

'*Why not*?'

'It's not our type of story, Nick. It's fucking *Sunday Times* stuff. Tits and arse, that's us.'

Mullen picked up a copy of the day's *Dispatch* from MacLeod's desk and jabbed his finger at the headline: UNION BULLY BOYS GOT US TO CHANGE OUR VOTES, WORKERS CLAIM. 'What the hell's that, then, Jack? D'you call that tits and arse?'

'No,' MacLeod said defensively. 'That's a human interest story.'

'So what the hell do you think *this* story's all about, eh, Jack? It's dripping with human interest, man! *Dripping* with it! A kid on the run disappears onto a top secret base, never to be seen alive again! I'll dress it up, Jack,' Mullen pleaded. 'I'll write it like a *Daily Dispatch* story, I promise you! I'll throw some tits and arse in for good measure. For crying out loud, Jack – can't you see it, man? It'll be a damn good exclusive for us!'

MacLeod's resistance was weakening. 'I'll have to talk to Arnold about it,' he waffled.

'And Arnold'll have to talk to the managing editor about it, and he'll have to talk to Victor Kingsbrook. Come on, Jack, give me a break. Let me do the work on it, read the copy and then make a decision.'

'Ah,' MacLeod said, shaking his head, 'you're a fucking nuisance.' He hesitated; Mullen waited for the assent he was sure was imminent. Just then the door opened and Arnold Reece breezed in. He nodded brusquely at Mullen and said, with his usual self-importance, 'I need to talk to you, Jack.'

Mullen remained seated, waiting. 'I'll let you know this afternoon,' MacLeod told him. 'The funeral's at four o'clock.' Mullen rose and walked to the door, taking his time. Reece looked him up and down with displeasure. 'Think you can manage a shave before then?' he called after him.

Chapter Seventeen

Swathed in a black Saville Row suit and false
humility, Sir Victor Kingsbrook – the *Dispatch*'s
proprietor – stood beside Bayliss's coffin, con-
cluding a eulogy Mullen knew would have sent
Bayliss, roaring with laughter, to the nearest
pub. 'And if there is one word that could sum
up the life and work of Vernon Bayliss,' Kingsbrook said, in the tones of a parent instructing
a very small child, 'it must be the word, professional. He was a dedicated newspaperman who was
always resolute in the pursuit of truth, hunting it
down without fear or favour, and in a humble
way, I am proud that I was able to give him the
opportunity to exercise his talents without restrict-
ion or interference. I am sure that our dear friend
and colleague would wish us all to maintain and
treasure – even to extend – the high standards of
journalism which were his watchword. May he rest
in peace.'

Clean-shaven and suitably attired in dark suit and

tie, Mullen sat with a contingent of other *Dispatch* people in the chapel of the Gardens of Rest. The small building was filled with reporters, editors, photographers, printers and secretaries from most of the papers in Fleet Street. Kingsbrook resumed his seat in the front row, amongst Bayliss's relatives. A minister took his place in the pulpit and recited a short prayer. To the sound of canned heavenly music, a purple velvet curtain opened electrically, as though by divine intervention, and the coffin passed on a small conveyor belt into some celestial recess behind the curtain, which closed after it. The minister cleared his throat loudly. 'If you would be good enough, ladies and gentlemen, to clear the chapel as soon as possible, as we have another service in five minutes – this would be appreciated. Also, may I draw your attention to the Hall of Wreaths, which is off to your right as you leave. Thank you.'

Obediently, people began to file out. As Mullen moved down the aisle, MacLeod tapped him on the shoulder. 'You haven't got enough,' he said, *sotto voce*, 'But it will be dynamite when you do . . . ' he pointed back toward the curtain with his thumb ' . . . and that old bugger will be laughing in his urn.'

'So I've got a go-ahead?'

'No guarantees,' MacLeod said pointedly.

'I know, Jack.'

A small group of people, apparently Bayliss's relatives, stood at the door, receiving condolences. Mullen considered going over to them, but couldn't think what he might say. As he edged past them and out the door, he recognized a woman in a long black coat and boots, her blonde hair pulled back severely with a black ribbon, moving towards the cars parked in the road. It was Nina Beckman, Markham's secretary. 'Miss Beckman!' he called. She turned, saw him, and quickened her pace. He began to run after her. 'Miss Beckman!'

'Mr Mullen!' an authoritative voice called out. It was Kingsbrook, leaning out the window of his Bentley. Mullen paused. 'Nick Mullen, isn't it?'

'Yes,' he said, watching Nina fumble for her keys beside a small red Renault.

'Victor Kingsbrook. How d'you do?' He stretched out his hand; Mullen had no choice but to shake it. 'Just wanted to congratulate you on that marvellous piece about Kleist and Markham. Terrific. What you working on now? Anything exciting?'

'Yes,' Mullen said, stumbling over his words. 'I'm . . . well, it's early days yet, but . . . '

'Well, never mind,' Kingsbrook said heartily. 'We'll read all about it, I expect, when you're ready.' He nodded at the chauffeur; the electric window slid shut and the Bentley moved off – just as Nina's Renault did the same. Gathering his wits about him, Mullen remembered his own car, parked a bit further up the road. He ran for it, jumped in and took off in pursuit of the Renault.

Cursing the rush hour traffic in the West End, he hooted wildly at drivers, who angrily let him pass. Nearing Trafalgar Square, he overtook a van, only to find himself behind Kingsbrook's Bentley. He could still glimpse the Renault, several cars ahead. The Bentley turned off at the Strand; Mullen followed the Renault past Nelson's Column and down Northumberland Avenue toward the river. Nina turned left onto the Embankment and parked, nose-first, just past Hungerford Bridge. Mullen skidded into the nearest parking space, jumped out of his car and ran along the Embankment, trying not to lose sight of Nina in the throng of pedestrians. Hearing him call her name, she hurried even faster – through the Underground Station and up the Hungerford Bridge steps. Out of breath, trying to make himself heard above the din of the trains hurtling in and out of Charing Cross Station, he shouted, 'Miss Beckman! I know about August the ninth!'

She stopped, turned and gave him an ice-cold glare that told him to keep his distance. He raised his hands in a gesture of surrender. 'Okay . . . I know you've got every reason not to trust me.'

'Give me one good reason why I should?'

'I know about the base?'

'So?'

Mullen fumbled in his pocket and brought out the draft of his article. She glared at him contemptuously for a moment, but couldn't resist reaching for the pages and scanning them. Mullen stood apprehensively, nervous, feeling like a schoolboy having sums checked. 'There are still some holes in it,' he explained. 'That's why I have to talk to Dennis Markham.'

Nina flicked to the last page and looked up. 'So you can get another tawdry front page under your belt?'

He grabbed for the article. 'If you can't set up a meeting, let's forget it.' He turned to move off.

'Mr Mullen,' she said, calling after him. 'Do you still think Dennis Markham is a spy?'

He turned back, confused. 'Jesus Christ, no! Of course not!'

'Then why the hell doesn't it say that here?'

He took a step toward her. 'Because . . . because if he isn't, that must mean he was framed, and I can't figure out how – '

'You didn't have a problem figuring out Prague,' she said sarcastically.

'Look . . . Prague was a mistake. I should have listened to Vernon. I need your help!' he entreated. 'I need your help.'

'Two weeks after your newspaper broke the story about Miranda Court and Kleist,' she said reproachfully, 'Dennis was due to have an Adjournment Debate. He was due to ask questions about the Dyce Affair that the Government simply would not have been able to duck. The story breaks: Dennis is forced to resign. No debate!'

'What questions? What questions was he going to ask?'

'Just one, basically: How close had East Anglia come to being a radioactive wasteland?'

Mullen stared at her, his worst suspicions confirmed; the impact of her words blocked out the

122

noise of the traffic and trains. Finally he said, 'I don't understand how Kleist and the KGB come into it. It doesn't make sense!'

'The only person who knew the answer to that question was Vernon. He had something, or was about to get something, which he said would prove a frame-up beyond any reasonable doubt . . . '

'Who's George?' Mullen interjected.

'George who?'

'I don't know – a contact – a friend of Vernon's . . . '

'George Paxton?'

'Posh voice and a stammer?' She shook her head. 'Damn. What about Markham? Would he know?'

'He might. But he's in a villa in the middle of Tuscany with his wife. There's no phone.'

'I could fly out!'

Nina shook her head emphatically. 'He just doesn't want to know any more, Mr Mullen.' She looked at her watch. 'Look, I'm sorry . . . I'm late. I've got to go . . . '

'Thanks for the information,' he said, gratefully. With the faintest of smiles, she turned away.

Mullen watched her cross the bridge, then looked around at the parade of pedestrians coming and going. Commuters hurried to catch their trains; tourists dawdled, gaping at the view of the river and St. Paul's. The lights of the South Bank complex promised an evening of music, theatre, cinema. The scene looked as picturesque and benign as an Andrew Murray greeting card. Mullen shivered as he turned back towards the Embankment. The same instincts that had told him that Lehane was lying were now telling him that he was being watched.

Chapter Eighteen

Back at his flat, his instincts were confirmed. His mail had been opened, then crudely resealed. Someone had tampered with his stereo system and moved the tone arm from its normal resting place onto the bare turntable. Either the spooks were incredibly sloppy, he thought, or else they were deliberately alerting him to their presence, trying to scare him. But the fear that had practically paralysed him when he'd heard them on his phone line was draining away now, replaced by an outrage that fuelled him as nothing, not even ambition, ever had.

He put the draft of his article on his desk and sat down. He opened a drawer, extracted two clear white sheets of paper, inserted some carbon between them and carefully rolled papers and carbon into the typewriter. He typed his name at the top and continued typing furiously, with two fingers, for most of the next three hours. 'On August 9th of last year . . . Detention Centre in Norfolk . . . Steven Dyce's body . . . villagers awakened in night . . . emergency alert . . . F1-11s armed with nuclear warheads . . . '

Just after nine o'clock he removed the last sheet of paper from his typewriter and stapled it together with the others. He did the same with the carbon copies, putting them in his desk drawer. He sealed the original pages in an envelope and drove with them across town, not even bothering to check for possible pursuers.

Leaving the BMW double-parked outside the *Dispatch* building, he ran inside, up the stairs, and burst into MacLeod's office, interrupting a meeting with two other newsmen. 'Talk to you in the morning, Jack,' he said, shoving the papers at the startled Scotsman. He drove straight home, fell into bed and tried, without much success to sleep. At least, he thought ruefully, waking from a dream in which F1-11s crashed all around him, my nightmares are unmistakably nightmares.

Mullen was back at the office at ten a.m., waiting in the carpeted corridor outside Arnold Reece's office for the regular morning editorial conference to end. Singly and in pairs, the heads of the paper's various desks emerged: sports, City, foreign, political, features, women, pictures. Finally MacLeod stuck his head out the door and beckoned to Mullen, who straightened his tie and walked nervously into the editor's office.

'Sorry to keep you,' Reece said. 'Pull up a pew.' Mullen sat down, relaxing slightly. 'What can I say? Terrific story. Strong. Colourful stuff. Congratulations.'

126

Mullen smiled warily. 'Thank you.'

'There is one problem, however,' Reece went on.
'What's that?'

Reece handed Mullen the original copy of his
story. 'I'm afraid we can't touch it, old son.'

Mullen looked over at MacLeod, standing
uncomfortably in the corner; no support from that
quarter, he could see. 'Why not?' he asked Reece
aggressively.

'The Official Secrets Act. They'd take us to the
cleaners.'

'But the Official Secrets Act is the whole bloody
point!' MacLeod shot Mullen a discreet look that
said, 'Keep your cool.'

'Kingsbrook doesn't wear it.'

'You showed it to Kingsbrook?'

'Seems he knew about it even before I did.' He
handed a letter across to Mullen. 'This was on my
desk when I arrived this morning.'

Mullen read it with dismay and disbelief: *Dear
Arnold, I have been informed that the Daily
Dispatch is at present in danger of facing charges
under the Official Secrets Act as a result of an
article which is being written or has already been
written by Mr Nicholas Mullen of our news staff
. . .* 'Jesus Christ! How the hell did he know?'

'Read on, dear boy,' Reece said.

*The practicalities of this appear to be that not
only Mr Mullen but also the editor, that is to say,
yourself are liable to prosecution. However, if we
refrain from publishing the story and Mullen
withdraws his active interest in it, the threat of*

prosecution will, I am assured, be lifted. Naturally there may be some element of bluff in all of this, but I feel it is my duty, nevertheless, to counsel extreme caution in this matter.

As you know, I am opposed in principle to any bludgeoning of the Free Press by government and, by the same token, it has been my custom as the Newspaper's Chairman to avoid interference in editorial policy. I feel, however, that an exception must be made in this case. From what I under- stand, it appears that Mr Mullen has touched upon matters which are severely injurious to the national interest and if this is truly the position, quite apart from the question of the Official Secrets Act, then I am afraid that I cannot allow his article to be associated with the Daily Dispatch or any of my newspapers. I reserve a final decision as soon as I am able to have sight of Mr Mullen's article.

'Obviously,' Reece broke in, 'I had to show it to Kingsbrook. The first thing he said was, "There's a lot of things wrong with this country, but it's not Bulgaria." ' He chuckled.

'He's put the block on it, Nick,' MacLeod said.

Mullen looked from MacLeod to Reece, and back to MacLeod. Two impotent wimps, he thought. Two gutless wonders. 'And you're both just going to let him walk all over you,' he said.

'I don't like it either, Nick,' Reece said placa- tingly, 'but we've all got the mortgage to think of.'

Mullen crumpled Kingsbrook's letter, threw it on the floor and left Reece's office, slamming the door behind him. He was halfway down the corridor when MacLeod caught up with him. 'Come on, man,' the Scotsman pleaded, 'be reasonable! What the hell did you expect Kingsbrook to do? Recommend you for an OBE? The man's into the Government for millions . . . '

'Who is?'

'Kingsbrook! Kingsbrook!'

Mullen stopped dead. '*What*?'

'Okay . . . Crozier Brown. You've heard of them?'

'The construction firm? Of course.'

'Well, Kingsbrook fucking owns it. Lock, stock and barrel.'

'But . . . what's the connection?'

'The connection is MOD building contracts – millions of pounds worth of them, mostly on American and British air force installations. Can't jeopardize them, old son.'

'Well,' said Mullen, fuming, 'you could have fucking told me!'

'Come on, man,' MacLeod said, 'be reasonable. It's not the first time you've had a story spiked.'

'It's the first time I've had a story like *this* one spiked. It's the first time I've *had* a story like this one, period!'

'I know, and you've made a damn good job of it, I'll say that.'

'Who the fuck does Kingsbrook think he is, anyway? National interest! Who's he to say what the national interest is? *I* think it's in the national interest that people should know about the strokes being pulled! They should be *told* what's fucking going on up there!'

MacLeod pulled Mullen into the nearest empty office and shut the door. 'Listen,' he said confidentially, 'I was the first man in Fleet Street to get a whiff of the Thorpe story. I knew about Norman Scott and Thorpe before anybody else on the street. And you know what happened? Hughes – that was before Kingsbrook's takeover – Hughes put the block on it – and then the self-same fucking story appeared in the *Mail* four weeks later. Jesus, what a sickener that was. See, we all get 'em, these knockbacks. You've got to learn to walk away from it and into the next story, and forget about the one that got away. And there's something else you want to think about as well – the Official Secrets Act. It's no joke, you know.'

Mullen snorted derisively. 'They'd never risk it. A public trial? You've got to be joking. All of this would have to come out into the open. If you guys had a bit more balls and went ahead and published, I'd lay good money we'd call their bluff.'

'Well,' MacLeod said, feigning nonchalance, 'if you want to try your luck with another paper, that's fine by me – but if you did that, I'd have to say you couldn't continue to work for the *Dispatch*.' He put a hand on Mullen's arm. 'Nick,' he said solicitously, 'have you taken a look at yourself lately? Being an enemy of the State really doesn't suit you, man. You look fucking terrible. What you need's a holiday. Look, get on a plane.

130

Spain, Portugal, Greece – anywhere there's a few easy birds and plenty of cheap booze. Take two weeks paid holiday in the sun. Either that or get a good night's kip, call me in the morning and start afresh. Whatever you fancy's fine with me.' He looked at his watch. 'I've got to go. Have a think about it, eh, Nick?'

Mullen spun around and mumbled something.

'What's that?'

'I said,' Mullen repeated loudly enough for half the newsroom to hear him, 'I just might not come back at all.'

Chapter Nineteen

Betrayal was the name of the game, all right, Mullen thought, driving back towards his flat, and everybody played it. Just as he had betrayed Trudy Markham, his bosses had now betrayed him. Kingsbrook didn't own him. He'd had enough of their paternalistic pats on the head and slaps on the wrist; he didn't need them. It was a good story, solid – even Reece had admitted that. There were plenty of other papers in town who would buy it. Hell, money wasn't even a consideration – he'd gladly *give* it away! The only consideration now was making the facts public, letting the public know what was really going on in those hallowed, hypocritical halls of government. He'd take his story, with Bayliss's photocopies and cassette, to the opposition. He spotted a brown Cortina in his rear view mirror. Paranoia be damned, he thought; I'll take on the whole bloody lot of you.'

He was not prepared, though for the sight that greeted him when he opened the door of his flat;

he had to lean against the door frame for support. The place had been savagely ransacked; it looked like a replay of Bayliss's flat the last time he'd seen it. The floor was piled with papers, books, the contents of drawers, overturned furniture. Even the back of the television set had been unscrewed. Pillows, cushions, even his duvet, had been ripped open; feathers were everywhere.

He rushed into the kitchen – and found the same devastation. The cupboards had been stripped of their contents; packets, containers and jars had been emptied onto the counters and floor. The fridge door gaped open, the orange juice carton gone. Mullen found it under some debris. Empty. Sick with rage, impotence and desolation, he punched a cabinet door with his fist. 'Bastards! You fucking bastards!'

The wreckage of his room was flooded with bright daylight when he opened his eyes the next morning, slightly hung over, a half dozen empty cans of McEwans beside his bed. He'd slept fitfully, still half-dressed from the previous day; in his dreams, faceless enemies stalked him down bombed-out streets that offered him no place to hide. He lay in his bed, surveying the shambles, all bravado gone. He reached for a cigarette and lit it; it tasted like compost, and he stubbed it out.

His head was throbbing, but he forced himself to consider his position. For the first time, he saw clearly how far beyond his depth he had ventured.

He was an amateur in the cloak-and-dagger world, where the professionals made the rules, and changed them to suit themselves. He was an inept babe in the woods, flirting with fires that he couldn't even identify. Even if his ego was as big as Margaret had claimed it was, he wasn't crazy enough to take on the entire system, official and covert.

What had they been after? It couldn't have been merely the photocopies and cassette; they weren't enough to incriminate anyone. What, he asked himself for the hundredth time, had they been after at Bayliss's flat? For the hundredth time, he came up blank.

He'd wind up like Bayliss, he thought, if he kept to this course; more than his career was at stake now. Much as he hated to admit it, MacLeod had been right; without evidence that proved Markham had been framed, the story just wouldn't hold up. Cut your losses, he told himself; you can't win this one. He picked up the phone, dialled the number of the *Dispatch* and waited.

'News desk,' he said groggily.

'News desk.'

'Jack there? It's Nick Mullen.'

MacLeod picked up his phone. 'Nick! How you feeling?'

'Okay. I'm coming in, Jack.'

'You sure? You sound a wee bit . . . '

'I'm fine,' Mullen said emphatically. 'Absolutely fine. You know how much I love my work, Jack.'

'Well suit yourself. See you later.' He hung up;

134

Mullen heard the telltale click on the line. He looked out at the apparently empty windows across the way. The walls have ears, he thought — what about eyes? He lowered the blinds.

He was scrubbing himself vigorously in the bath, beginning to feel faintly human again, not listening to the radio he had automatically turned on. 'In a move which has become increasingly familiar in cases of this kind,' the newscaster was saying, 'the Magistrate ordered the blacking out of Courtroom windows and exclusion of reporters. John Chillingham was outside the Court.'

Another voice — Chillingham's — took over. 'George Rydell is no ordinary Civil Servant. He is in the highly secretive Home Office Department called F4, whose function Rydell himself described when called to give evidence at a recent Commons Select Committee hearing on the activities of the Special Branch.' Chillingham's voice gave way to the unmistakable sound of a recording from the Commons Select Committee hearings: coughs, fidgets, the shuffling of papers and, in the middle of it, the echo of a man's voice speaking in a large, cavernous room.

'The Department has, in essence, a threefold responsibility,' the voice said. Something about it riveted Mullen's attention. 'It is responsible for Public Order for issues related to the arming of the police and for liaison with both Special Branch and M15.' The voice had the same distinctive stammer and cut-glass accent that Mullen had listened to dozens of times on Bayliss's microcassette.

Chillingham continued. 'Even though this is only a preliminary hearing, the government is clearly taking the case very seriously indeed. Yet apart from the charges, themselves, which are under both Sections One and Two of the Official Secrets Act, no mention has been made of the sixty-year-old Civil Servant's offence. From a statement issued by Mr Rydell's solicitors today, there is an indication that a document allegedly leaked to the press is involved . . . '

Mullen was out of the bath and, still dripping, trying to get into his clothes. He knew what he had to look for now; and he had remembered where it was.

Chapter Twenty

Mullen waited impatiently as the lift, an old-fashioned grille type, creaked at a snail-like pace up to the floor of Bayliss's flat. He slid the gate back and cautiously walked the few steps to the front door. It was ajar; he heard muffled voices coming from inside. Trembling, he pushed the letter-box open and peered through the slot. Two pairs of feet – men's feet – were pacing back and forth across the floor.

The floor has been stripped of its carpet. They must still be searching, Mullen thought – if they'd found what they were looking for, they wouldn't still be here. He ran down the stairs to the landing where Bayliss had stood on that dreadful night, and looked where, he now realized, Bayliss had looked – up the lift shaft. Through the wire mesh of the cage, he could see only shadows. Was that a bulge under the ledge of the landing, or just his imagination?

He crept quietly back up the stairs and slid the

lift gate open. Every squeak echoed in his head like thunder, but the door to the flat remained only slightly ajar. He pressed the 'Down' button and pressed his face against the gate, looking up. One floor down, he passed it – a foolscap manila envelope, securely taped to the underside of the ledge. He pressed the 'Emergency Stop' button and stared at the envelope. 'Vernon,' he whispered, 'you cunning old bugger!'

He pressed the 'Up' button and then, almost immediately, the emergency stop again. He was close enough now to poke his hand through the gate and reach for the envelope. Without any warning, the lift started down again. He pulled his hand in, an instant before it would have been crushed. Trying desperately to think clearly, caught between the dangers above and below, he pushed the emergency stop button again. Still between floors, he opened the gate a few feet, to prevent any further surprise movements. The envelope seemed just out of reach; straining, he managed to touch it, then struggled to free it from the tape that held it in place. Vernon had done a thorough job; there seemed to be masses of tape. A sound echoed faintly from the depths of the silent building. Footsteps, far below on the stairs. Climbing. Coming closer.

In a panic, drenched with sweat, he pulled desperately at the corner of the envelope. As it finally came away from the tape, it slipped out of his damp fingers and down the shaft. He heard the faint noise at it landed on the bottom of the well.

So did the person on the stairs, whose footsteps stopped, then began to descend.

As slowly and gently as possible, Mullen slid the lift door open and climbed out. He crept down the stairs, scarcely daring to breathe. One landing. Then another. Nearly at the bottom, he squinted down through the grille to the base of the lift shaft and was barely able to make out a figure. Whoever it was was reaching through the cage toward the envelope that lay on the floor. As he reached the landing at the ground floor, the person below looked up at him with terrified eyes. It was Nina Beckman.

'What the hell are you doing here?' he asked, weak with relief.

'I heard about George Rydell.'

Mullen looked down at the envelope that still lay at the base of the lift shaft. They heard footsteps, this time from above, and the sound of the lift beginning to move. Mullen knelt and stretched his arm through the narrow opening. The envelope was just out of his reach. The lift was descending, coming closer. Nina pushed him aside and reached toward the envelope. Her arm, slimmer than his, stretched farther – just far enough. She pulled the envelope out as the lift ground to a halt, just above them.

Mullen saw a dark corner – a tradesman's entrance, perhaps – and pulled Nina into its shadows. They heard the gate of the lift open and close, and the sound of footsteps leaving the building. Without a word, Nina tore open the envelope and pulled out a sheaf of documents. She scanned them quickly and handed them to Mullen, a look of utter amazement on her face. Watching him read them, she touched his hand. 'You're shaking.'

Mullen stared, dumbfounded. The dossier was stamped TOP SECRET and labelled DIETRICH KLEIST. The Soviet spy whose alleged association with Dennis Markham had forced the MP's resignation was, in fact, a double agent – in the pay of the British since 1976.

The lift started to move again. 'We'd better get out of here,' Nina said. 'My car's outside. You wait here and I'll bring it round the back.'

'Just check that there's no one out there,' Mullen said, remembering the Cortina.

'Give me five minutes,'

In less than three minutes, the Renault pulled up to the kerb and Mullen got in. 'Where are we going?' Nina asked. 'Your paper?'

He shook his head. 'It's too hot. The *Dispatch* will never run the story. Not as long as Kingsbrook's in control.'

'Why not?'

'The story has to come from outside Fleet Street,' Mullen said. 'I'll explain later. What we've got to do now is find a photocopying machine. Trust me, Nina. Please.'

Seeing his obvious distress, her last qualms about him melted. 'What do you want me to do?'

He gave her some brief, very simple instructions.

Chapter Twenty-One

Mullen moved through the busy newsroom with such urgency that MacLeod, standing at the news desk, watched him with alarm. At his desk in the back row, Harry Champion, oblivious to Mullen's approach, sat, typing copy. 'Harry!' Nick said, loudly enough to attract the attention of the reporters who hadn't noticed him already. 'I want to talk to you!'

'My dear chap,' Champion said condescendingly, 'of course . . . '

Mullen looked round at their curious colleagues and pointed to the picture library; through its glass door, he could see that it was empty. 'In private.'

Reluctantly, Champion stood up; Mullen hustled him into the picture library and shut the door. Champion relaxed into a chair – looking, Mullen thought, sanctimonious as all hell. Mullen wasted no time on preliminaries. 'Where did the Markham tip-off come from, Harry?' he asked.

'Markham?' Champion replied flippantly. 'The

world's moved on since then, in case you hadn't noticed, old bean. We've had England lose another Test, riots in South London . . . '

Mullen prodded him in the chest with his fore-finger. 'Don't patronize me, *old bean*. Where did you get the tip-off?'

Champion hesitated. 'You know perfectly well I've got to protect my sources.'

'Yeah? Well from now on, Harry, nobody is protecting anybody any more.'

'I can't tell you,' Champion said, nervously looking through the glass door for reinforcements.

'I want to know,' Nick said, deadly serious, 'who told you Kleist was KGB?'

'I can't tell you.'

'It was the same source that rang me up and gave me the Prague story, wasn't it?'

'I've no idea.' Champion was looking every-where except into Mullen's eyes.

'Come on, Harry,' Nick said, softening a bit, coaxing.

'Look . . . he's in the Security Services. Very, very high up. I've used him for fifteen years and he's never been wrong. That's all I can tell you.'

'Oh, yeah? Well, it's time you got yourself a new contact, Harry – '

'I don't know what you're talking about . . . '

' . . . because Kleist is no more KGB than Philby was MI6. He's a British agent!'

Champion laughed derisively. 'That's very good? Where did you get that from, John LeCarré?'

'No, Harry. I got it from George Rydell. In

142

black and white.' He slammed the Kleist file into Champion's chest. Looking as though a bucket of cold water had been dumped on him, Champion scanned the papers in the file. 'I want a name, Harry.'

Cornered, Champion capitulated. 'Clegg. Anthony Clegg.'

'Where is he?'

Mullen parked his car in Pall Mall and reached under the front seat for his attaché case. He opened it, fished his tiny tape recorder out of the mess of papers, checked the batteries and inserted a cassette. With the recorder in his pocket, he walked toward the grand and formal Victorian building. Several black Princess Limousines were parked near the imposing facade. He followed an elderly man in a camel's hair coat up the steps to the revolving doors. A doorman moved quickly to block his way. 'Yes, sir, can I help you?'

'Anthony Clegg. Is he in?'

'Yes, sir.' The doorman moved toward a phone. 'Who shall I say . . . ?'

'Reece,' Mullen said, right off the top of his head. 'Arnold Reece.'

'From?' He picked up the phone.

'F4. Home Office.'

As the doorman turned away to make the call, Mullen slipped into the hall and made for a central staircase. At the top, he followed a passageway past rooms as sombre and still as mausoleums. In the library, a high-ceilinged room lined with Anti-quarian books, a walruslike member sat quietly, reading. 'You haven't seen Anthony Clegg, by any chance, have you?'

The walrus looked up. 'I think you'll find him in the Main Lounge.' He returned to his reading.

The Main Lounge was a large, thickly carpeted room with military paintings on the walls – mementoes of Imperial conquests. Between the door and the bar at the far end of the room stretched a sea of leather armchairs, most of them occupied by middle-aged and elderly men – the high echelons of the military and defence establishment at their leisure.

Mullen removed his raincoat and draped it over his arm, wondering which of them was Clegg. A white-coated waiter passed in front of him, carrying a tray of coffee. 'Excuse me,' Nick said politely, 'Is Anthony Clegg in?'

'That's him there, sir . . . standing up.' He pointed across the room, over the heads of the other members, to a tall, grey-haired man in his mid-fifties getting up from an armchair and starting to walk in his direction. Mullen watched him intently, trying to place the face. Clegg walked closer; he stopped beside a pillar to greet another member and then suddenly seemed to disappear in the crowd of men. Mullen stepped forward to confront him. 'Anthony Clegg?' Clegg looked dispassion-ately at him. 'I'm Nick Mullen.' Clegg was a cool one: his expression revealed nothing at all. 'We spoke on the phone, remember?'

144

Clegg kept his composure, showing no sign of recognition whatsoever. Mullen hesitated, momentarily thrown. Could this be the wrong man? Clegg held his gaze, then slowly raised his eyes from Mullen's to something, or someone, behind him, breaking the spell. 'I think there must be some mistake,' he said haughtily.

Mullen was about to speak when a voice behind him said, 'Mr Mullen?' He spun around to see three men gliding silently from out of nowhere, positioning themselves around him. The one who stood between him and the Main Lounge held out a badge. 'We are police officers,' he said. 'We have reason to believe that offences have been committed under the Official Secrets Act.'

Mullen turned back toward Clegg, who stood like a monolith, untouchable. 'You bastard!' The policemen grabbed his arms. He tried to pull himself away, but against the three of them, he hadn't a chance. 'Was it a heart attack?' he shouted as the police dragged him away. The members looked on, idly curious about the intrusion into their sanctum sanctorum. In a moment, the disturbance had subsided; order and equilibrium were restored.

Chapter Twenty-two

The police marched Mullen out of the Main Lounge, down the staircase, across the main foyer of the club, past a confused doorman, through the revolving doors and out onto the steps. At the bottom of the steps, several more plain-clothes police officers stood beside two unmarked cars, double-parked, doors flung open. Mullen was escorted down the steps into one of the cars: a brown Cortina.

'They think this is the end of it, but it's just the beginning,' Mullen thought, feeling a surge of hope as the car sped down the Mall, past Trafalgar Square. If Nina had carried out their plan . . .

At that moment, Nina was standing in a long, seemingly motionless queue at the main Post Office, holding a large manila envelope addressed to the editor of *Le Monde*, in Paris. She waited impatiently, tapping her foot; an eternity passed before she reached the front of the queue. The man ahead of her appeared to be settling his entire estate. At last he moved away and she stepped up to the window. She put the envelope on the scale. The clerk gave her a form to fill out for Recorded Delivery. He took her money, gave her a receipt and the envelope disappeared behind the counter. Buoyant with relief, Nina walked away, looking straight ahead, her heels clicking on the marble floor.

Behind her, a woman stepped up to the window she'd left and flashed her credentials at the clerk. 'Police,' she said tersely. 'The envelope you just accepted is stolen property.' She showed him a warrant. Minutes later, the spook was leaving, the envelope tucked underneath her arm.

Chapter Twenty-three

A tall, fiftyish man in a smart pin-stripe suit emerged from a building in Whitehall as the Cortina pulled up to the kerb. 'How d'you do, Mr Mullen,' he said, extending his hand. 'My name is Richard Leith. I'm an Under Secretary here.' Bewildered, Mullen shook his hand. 'I believe you have an appointment.'

'First I've heard of it,' said Mullen. 'I mean, if I'd known, I'd have worn a tie . . . '

'I wouldn't worry unduly about that, Mr Mullen,' said Leith, missing the sarcasm. 'I'll take you to the Conference Room.' He ushered Mullen inside the building, up an ornate Baroque staircase and along a deserted corridor. He stopped before a large wooden door and knocked. 'Come,' a magisterial voice commanded. The Ministry man opened the door, motioned Mullen inside and shut the door behind him.

It was a very long room, dimly lit. The walls

were panelled with oak and hung with oils – Old Masters – that added to the gloom. At the far end of the room, a good fifty feet from where Mullen stood, three men sat at a long, bare table, their faces reflected in its polished surface. A huge canvas of an eighteenth – or nineteenth-century battle covered most of the wall behind them. 'Good evening, Mr Mullen,' said the man in the middle, gesturing toward a straight-backed leather chair. 'Please sit down.'

Mullen walked nervously toward the men, thinking of the three brass monkeys: See No Evil, Hear no Evil, Speak No Evil. They all looked in their early sixties – relaxed, urbane, accustomed to wielding power. He fiddled uncertainly with the chair. 'Please be seated,' the man repeated. He seemed to be the spokesman for the tribunal – or whatever it was. 'Let me apologize,' he went on, 'for the precipitate way in which you were brought here.'

'What is this – a trial?' Mullen asked. 'Am I under arrest?'

'Lord, no. Not yet . . . '

Mullen considered the implication. 'Has no one explained the position to you, Mr Mullen?' the man on the left asked him.

Mullen shook his head. 'No one's explained damn-all.'

'Well, in that case, Mr Mullen, we owe you an apology.' See No Evil continued. 'Really, we simply would like to have a friendly chat with you. We are assessors, here to assess your case – '

149

'What case?'

' – and make recommendations as to action – '

'*What* case?'

'I may add that nothing that is said within these walls carries any legal weight, Mr Mullen, and if any notes are taken by any one of us they are simply by way of being an aide-memoire, nothing more. Well, perhaps we could start now . . . '

'*What bloody case*?' Mullen exploded. The men were silent, their faces expressionless.

'You are a very intriguing person, Mr Mullen,' Hear No Evil said at last. He looked at some notes in a dossier in front of him. 'No background of politics in your family . . . no involvement with politics during your youth, apart from a brief fling in 1968. Not even a member of the Campaign for Nuclear Disarmament. You don't appear to have unpatriotic leanings of any kind.'

'If you don't mind my asking,' said the man on the left, 'how did you vote at the last General Election?'

'I didn't.'

'I see.' He jotted something on his notepad, the scratching of his pen echoing in the cavernous room and in Mullen's head, as well. 'May we know why?'

'No, you may not know why!'

'You felt yourself to be superior to the general mob, did you?'

Mullen snorted his disgust. The man in the middle took over. 'Given your political history, or lack of it, it is particularly bewildering to us to hear

150

that you now appear intent on a course of action that is potentially so damaging to the country's interests.'

'Is it the country's interests or yours that we're talking about?'

The remark was ignored. 'Mr Mullen, do you consider yourself a patriot?'

'Oh, come on – what kind of question is that?'

'A perfectly straightforward one, I should have thought, Mr Mullen. Do you consider yourself a patriot?' Mullen thought of Kafka, and said nothing. 'From what we can gather, you don't seem to have any especially unpatriotic leanings, Mr Mullen. You would agree, would you not, that certain things bearing on the defence of the realm are best left unsaid?'

'If you mean covered up, I don't.'

'From that I take it that you are a believer in the freedom of information.'

'Yes.'

'*All* information?' the man on the left interjected. 'Freely available, over the counter? If you discovered that there was some childishly simple way of, for example, stealing a nuclear bomb, would you simply go ahead and write about it?'

'Oh, come on, you know very well that's a completely different matter.'

'But where precisely do you draw the line, Mr Mullen? Where would you stop, once you embark on this striptease of a government?'

'I don't know. You're the guys who draw the lines, not me.'

'*We* don't draw the lines. The lines are drawn by a consensus of opinion, a *democratic* consensus of opinion.'

'Democratic? Don't make me laugh. How can you call it democracy when you only throw people the titbits of information you want to throw them? Your precious secrecy – that's how you hold on to power!'

The man's face showed just the slightest annoyance. 'By all accounts you *are* a loyal subject, Mr Mullen, but it would appear that you are perfectly happy to impart information that gives aid and sustenance to our enemies. You described, in some detail, how a mere boy managed to penetrate the high-security zone of an airbase dedicated to the defence of your country. Do you really think it's in the country's interests that such a thing should be made public?'

'The boy was killed! His body was dumped by the roadside. We came *that close* to a nuclear disaster!' Another silence – this one colder, more menacing. 'Are you going to stop me the same way you stopped Bayliss? Are you going to dump my body by the roadside, like Dyce's?'

The pen of the man on the left continued to scratch on the notepad. The man on the right spoke for the first time. 'I am instructed that any action against you will be dropped if you agree to refrain from further involvement in this matter.'

Mullen pondered his legal position – ambiguous, at best. He looked at the members of this strange, self-appointed tribunal, with its incalculable power over the country that he did love, but in a way they could never understand. He considered that the wrong answer could mean that he'd never be seen or heard from again. He thought about Bayliss, of Dennis and Trudy Markham, of Nina Beckman and Steven Dyce. He thought of films he'd seen in which he'd found scenes like this one completely unbelievable. His throat felt tight, his mouth dry. 'I'll see you in court,' he said.

The Three Brass Monkeys regarded him reproachfully. 'Are we to understand, then,' said Hear No Evil, 'that you intend to pursue this story?'

Mullen cleared his throat. 'Yes.'

'Sorry, what did you say, Mr Mullen?'

'Yes!' His voice boomed around the room. 'I said yes, I do intend to pursue this story.'

The echo of his words died away, replaced by a wall of silence. 'I'm sorry to hear you say that, Mr Mullen. Thank you for your time.' The Chairman rose, indicating that the interview, if that was what it had been, was over.

'Is that all?' Nick asked, confused. 'I'm free to leave?'

'For the moment, Mr Mullen. The gentleman at the door will see you out.'

As though in response to some secret signal, the door opened and Leith, the Ministry man, reappeared. Mullen walked toward him, then whirled back in the direction of the 'advisers', who were gathering their things together. *What really killed Vernon Bayliss?* he shouted, his voice carrying all

153

the frustration, grief and anger of the past week.
In the wall behind the men, another door opened.
Wordlessly, they filed through it; silently, it closed
behind them.

Chapter Twenty-four

The three policemen who had brought Mullen to the Ministry were waiting for him outside the Conference Room. They surrounded him with military precision; 'This way, sir,' one of them said.

'They told me I'm free to go' Mullen said indignantly.

'This way, sir,' the man repeated. Mullen had no choice but to comply. Was he still in custody after all? They moved through a maze of corridors, apparently toward the back of the building this time. Mullen was beyond fear now; he felt curiously calm and fatalistic. As they passed a glass door that seemed to lead into still another hallway, Mullen could see another group of officials escorting someone in the opposite direction. He got a fleeting glimpse of the other 'prisoner'. It was Nina Beckman. His heart sank like a stone.

He turned instinctively to follow her but the policemen surrounded him tightly and moved him along still another corridor that ended at the door to a lift. Gently but firmly they eased him into the enclosure. A button was pressed. The door closed.

Confined in the cramped, coffinlike space with the grim-faced policemen, Mullen's fatalism evaporated. The old-fashioned lift hit the bottom of its shaft with a shuddering bump. The doors opened and Mullen stepped out, sweating, expecting the men to accompany him. Instead, the doors closed and he was alone in a huge, dark, silent carpark.

He made out a pinpoint of light across the expanse of darkness and took a step towards it. He heard, or thought he heard, a sound behind him. Looking back, he saw only darkness. He took one hesitant step, then another. He stopped, thinking he'd heard a footfall, and looked back, half expecting a bullet to tear through his body from out of the darkness. He heard nothing but the sound of his pounding heart. Tentatively, he made his way toward the exit, and into the early evening light.

Mullen walked aimlessly through the rain, trying to clear his head, to make some sense of the surreal interrogation. Was Nina even now being made to jump through the same bizarre hoops. They must have caught up with her before she'd been able to post the envelope – otherwise, they would never have let her go. It had been an impossible plan, anyway – they'd been crazy to think they had a chance in hell of getting away with it. For the first

156

time in days, the sensation that someone was tailing him was gone. It was over. They knew he was no longer a threat.

His flat was just as he'd left it that morning – it seemed a year ago – when he'd heard Rydell's voice on the radio and rushed off to Bayliss's flat. He stood in the wreckage feeling drained, defeated, profoundly depressed. Miraculously, the one thing in the room that seemed not to have been disturbed was his record player. He dug out the Pachelbel Canon, the most soothing music he knew, and put it on the turntable. The sound filled the room, heartbreakingly beautiful, transcending all treachery and despair. Mullen was unmoved. He tried to think of one person he trusted who would believe him if he asked for help, and came up blank.

The sound of the doorbell punctuated the music. He froze, then walked warily to the door. 'Who is it?'

Nina couldn't wait to tell Nick how well it had gone – exactly according to plan! The spook had followed her to the Post Office, even stood right behind her in the queue, eyeing the envelope addressed to *Le Monde*. Nina hadn't looked back until she reached the street; then, backtracking to make sure she'd eluded any possible pursuers, she practically ran to a small Post Office Substation in a stationer's a few streets away. There, she posted another envelope, this one to a West German address. She wondered how long it had taken the spook to discover that the *Le Monde* envelope contained only blank sheets of paper.

The police had been waiting for her at her flat, but the trip to the Ministry had been a pointless exercise. Once they'd realized what she'd done, they had no recourse but to let her go.

Mullen opened the door cautiously; he looked haggard and ashen, but infinitely relieved to see her. She gave him a radiant, triumphant smile. 'Nick, we've done it!'

The magnificent chords of the canon soared through the room, a testament to the ultimate triumph of the human spirit. Exultant, Mullen reached out to embrace Nina. As he did, the music was obliterated by the sound of a massive explosion that instantly engulfed the room in an enormous ball of flame.

Epilogue

Driving to work the next morning, Jack MacLeod wondered, not for the first time, what the hell was going on with Nick Mullen, and why he was so obsessed with the story Kingsbrook had spiked. And why, for that matter, he'd never shown up yesterday after he'd phoned to say he was coming in. Mullen was getting too cocky for his own good. He wasn't a kid any more; it was time he learned, as MacLeod had had to learn, that everything had its price, and life was compromise. To get along, you had to go along.

He reached for the dial on his car radio and tuned in to Radio One to catch the news. He'd missed all but the final item: 'Emergency services report that at least one person has died and two others were injured in a gas explosion which occurred early this morning in a block of flats in central London. Eye witnesses remember seeing a postman delivering a parcel. He apparently told an elderly woman resident that he could smell gas and thought she should call the Gas Board and vacate the premises.' A slow news day, MacLeod thought. He switched it off, drove into the *Dispatch's* car park, pulled into his parking space and hurried into the building. He was on his way to the editorial meeting, hoping they hadn't started without him, when he noticed the crowd of newsmen clustered around the tele-text machine. 'Bloody hell, Jack,' one of them said, ' . . . take a look at this!'

He stopped, stared at the lead paragraph and watched, incredulous, as the machine tapped out the story:

'A report published yesterday in the German newspaper *Suddeutsche Zeitung* implicates the British Government in an attempt to conceal information concerning a near-nuclear accident on an American air base in Britain. The report goes on to say that British Security Services used a double agent, Dietrich Kleist, in an attempt to create a scandal involving Opposition MP, Dennis Markham. The article claims that the government's successful attempt to destroy the political career of Dennis Markham was intended to prevent his asking questions in the House of Commons regarding the incident and the death of Steven Dyce, a runaway from the Campton Youth Detention Centre, whose body was dumped by a roadside after being hit by an F1-11 aircraft during a NATO alert . . . '